"I've thought a lo... Tallulah," he said **...one thing."**

Her eyes wide with surprise, she made a slow study of his face. "Running away?"

"Okay. Maybe I regret two things," he answered gently. "Running away. And not doing this."

Her smile was like sunshine and for the first time in years he felt the cold spots inside him begin to warm.

"You mean staying long enough to drink coffee and talk with me?"

"More than that."

As if he'd lost control of his body, his uninjured hand reached out and curved around the warm flesh of her shoulder at the same time his face drew nearer and nearer to hers. Until suddenly all he could see was the fascinating shape of her lips.

"Jim."

His name floated out on a soft whisper and the sound was so erotic it caused him to groan.

"I should've kissed you the other night, Tallulah. I wanted to taste your lips. But I was afraid to."

"Why were you afraid? Did you think I wouldn't kiss you back?"

"No. I was afraid I'd like it—far too much."

Dear Reader,

When Tallulah O'Brien decides to move to Arizona and become the new nanny on Three Rivers Ranch, finding a man to give her a home and children is not in her plans. She'd already had one man and he'd been a stinker. Why would she want another? As for kids, she had plenty of Hollister children to mother; she didn't need her own. At least, that's what she tells herself. But as soon as she meets head horse groom Jim Carroway her wishes for the future take a sharp turn. Could he be the true soul mate she'd often dreamed about?

After working many years on Three Rivers Ranch, Jim lived a comfortable but uneventful life. And that's exactly the way he wanted it to be. He'd already suffered through the tragedy of losing a young wife and child to an accident. He never intended to set himself up for that sort of grief again. So why was he giving the new ranch nanny a closer look? And why was he beginning to wish he had the courage to reach for the love his lonely heart craves?

I've always loved second-chance stories. After all, getting up from a hard fall and trying again is what life is all about. I hope you enjoy reading how Jim and Tallulah finally realize how blessed they are to find a second chance in each other.

God bless the trails you ride,

The Wrangler Rides Again

STELLA BAGWELL

◆H HARLEQUIN
SPECIAL
EDITION

HARLEQUIN®

SPECIAL
EDITION™

ISBN-13: 978-1-335-40842-6

The Wrangler Rides Again

Harlequin Enterprises ULC
22 Adelaide St. West, 41st Floor
Toronto, Ontario M5H 4E3, Canada
www.Harlequin.com

Printed in U.S.A.

Recycling programs
for this product may
not exist in your area.

After writing more than one hundred books for Harlequin, **Stella Bagwell** still finds it exciting to create new stories and bring her characters to life. She loves all things Western and has been married to her own real cowboy for forty-four years. Living on the south Texas coast, she also enjoys being outdoors and helping her husband care for the horses, cats and dog that call their small ranch home. The couple has one son, who teaches high school mathematics and is also an athletic director. Stella loves hearing from readers. They can contact her at stellabagwell@gmail.com.

Books by Stella Bagwell

Harlequin Special Edition

Men of the West

The Rancher's Best Gift
Her Man Behind the Badge
His Forever Texas Rose
The Baby That Binds Them
Sleigh Ride with the Rancher

Montana Mavericks: The Real Cowboys of Bronco Heights

For His Daughter's Sake

The Fortunes of Texas: The Lost Fortunes

Guarding His Fortune

Montana Mavericks: The Lonelyhearts Ranch

The Little Maverick Matchmaker

Visit the Author Profile page at Harlequin.com for more titles.

To cowboys, horses and all things Western!
And to all the readers who've followed my
Men of the West series over the years. Thank you!

Chapter One

"Oh, darn it!"

Tallulah O'Brien muttered the words under her breath as a loud pop, coupled with a violent tug on the steering wheel, announced trouble.

Easing the SUV to a stop on the side of the dirt road, she set the parking brake and reached for the cell phone lying in a cup holder on the console.

"Why are we stopping, Nanny Tally?"

The question from Andrew Hollister prompted Tallulah to glance over her shoulder at the four young children safely strapped in their car seats. Andrew and his twin sister, Abagail, were situated on the seat directly behind Tallulah's while the second bench seat held little Evelyn and her younger brother, Billy.

"Let's get out and pick sagebrush," Abagail suggested before Tallulah could explain the sudden halt. "Mommy likes the flowers."

"I'm thirsty. I wanta drink," Billy, the youngest of the children, bemoaned from his seat at the back of the vehicle. "I don't wanta pick flowers!"

With the cell phone in hand, Tallulah turned and peered between the bucket seats at the impatient children.

"Okay, everyone. We're not getting out of the car to pick flowers," Tallulah said. "I'm going to step outside and while I do, I need for each of you to stay buckled in your seats just as you are. Understand?"

Evelyn immediately responded with a question. "What are you going to do outside, Nanny Tally? It's hot out there. And Daddy sees rattlers on the road all the time. If you got bit you'd be sick."

"No, Evie, people die when they get bit by a rattler." Abagail corrected her younger cousin, as though she was the snake authority of the group.

"You're dumb, Abby!" Andrew shot back at his twin sister. "Rattlers don't kill people. Not all the time."

From the back seat, Billy began to wail. "I don't want a snake to get me! I wanta go home!"

Under different circumstances, Tallulah would've been struggling not to laugh at the children's banter. But being stranded in the Arizona heat, with four youngsters in her care, took all the amusement out of the situation.

"Now, now. Let's not have any more talk about snakes," she said to the group, all of whom were looking expectantly at her. "Andy, you're good at telling stories. Tell one now. Just not the scary one about the owl."

"Okay. I'll tell them about Cletus the coyote," Andrew happily agreed.

While the boy began the story, Tallulah climbed out of the vehicle to confirm what she'd already suspected. A blowout had created a large hole in the side of the right front tire. With jagged pieces of rubber hanging in all direction, it was obvious a can of flat fixer would be useless on this catastrophe.

With a silent groan, she glanced from the ruined tire to the empty dirt road leading to the main headquarters of Three Rivers Ranch. On either side of the road, as far as the eye could see, the terrain was rough with slabs of rocks interspersed with agave, tall cacti, clumps of tough grass and a few Joshua trees. And even though it was only the first week in March, the sun was baking everything beneath its hot rays, including her.

Less than twenty minutes ago, she'd collected the children at a rural crossroad, where a special bus for preschoolers dropped them off at a designated spot located some ten miles from the ranch house. Fifteen more minutes and Reeva and Sophia would be expecting the children to enter the kitchen for their after-school snack. When she and the kids failed to show, worry bells would start to ring, along with Tallulah's cell phone.

Adjusting her sunglasses on her nose, Tallulah turned her back to the glare of the sun and scanned through the contact numbers on her phone. Just as she was about to punch the number to the ranch house kitchen, she caught the sound of an approaching vehicle coming from the direction of the main highway.

Glancing up, Tallulah spotted a white work truck with the ranch's 3R brand on the side. The sight caused a breath of relief to rush past her lips. Thank God, it was someone from the ranch, she thought, as she stood next to the fender of the SUV and waited for the truck to pull alongside.

When the darkened window on the passenger side lowered, she could see a man with rugged features, tawny blond hair, and a brown cowboy hat pulled low on his forehead sitting behind the steering wheel.

Leaning toward the open window, he peered out at her. "Having trouble?"

Shoving back a wave of dark, wind-tossed hair, she stepped toward the truck. "I'm afraid so. The right front tire has blown and I have four young children inside. I'm Tallulah O'Brien, by the way. The Hollisters' nanny."

The man quickly opened the driver's door and swung to the ground. When he skirted the front of the truck and joined her in the middle of the road, Tallulah struggled not to stare.

She'd only been living on Three Rivers for a short time. There were many ranch hands she'd never seen before, much less been introduced to. This one was definitely not average. Compared to her five foot five inches, he had to be over six feet, with a solid build that was emphasized by very faded denim jeans and a snapped Western shirt. His darkly tanned face was dominated by a pair of blue, blue eyes and a faint dimple in his left cheek.

"I'm James Garroway," he introduced himself. "Head wrangler for Three Rivers."

"Nice to meet you, James." She extended her hand to him and felt an instant jolt as his rough palm slid against hers.

"Pleasure meeting you, Ms. O'Brien. Call me Jim. Everybody does."

His voice had a deep, raspy timbre that was totally masculine. The sound of it, coupled with his striking features, momentarily scrambled her senses.

She cleared her throat and tried to look away from him, but the attempt failed as her gaze refused to budge from his face. "All right—Jim," she managed to say. "And I'd be happy for you to call me Tallulah."

"You must be Tag's sister," he said, while releasing his hold on her hand.

His blue eyes closely matched the bright sky, and right at this moment those vivid eyes were making a lazy inspection of her face. The idea that he was studying her so closely made her painfully aware of her tousled hair and bare lips. He was probably thinking she looked wrung out, Tallulah decided. But what did that matter? She expected he had a wife and family at home. And she wasn't regarding him in that way. Not in the least!

"I am Tag's sister," she replied. "I moved out here to the ranch about three weeks ago."

A faint smile touched his chiseled lips. "Welcome to Three Rivers Ranch," he said, then turned his focus on the SUV.

She let out a breath she hadn't realized she was holding. "I was about to call the ranch house for help when I heard your truck," she said. "If you're running short on time and need to be on your way, I'm sure Blake will send someone else to change the tire."

He moved to the front of the SUV and surveyed the problem. "No need for you to do that. I'm here and have the necessary tools in my truck."

"I'd be ever so grateful," she told him. "Do I need to get the children out of the vehicle?"

"No. Just make sure the parking brake is on before I start to jack it up."

"I've already done that," she told him. "But maybe I should open the windows and kill the engine while you work. Just to keep things safe. The children are strapped in, and I've ordered them to remain in their seats. But with three- and four-year-old kids, one never knows."

"Good idea," he said with a wry grin. "One of them might decide to try driving."

While she opened the windows on the SUV and cut the engine, the wrangler collected a high lift jack and a portable power wrench from the back of the work truck.

"That's Uncle Jim," Andrew declared as he leaned toward the open window as far as the seat belt would allow. "Are we gonna ride home with him?"

"Yippee! I want to ride in Uncle Jim's truck!" Evelyn chimed in. "He'll drive fast!"

Obviously the children were well acquainted with Jim Garroway. Which told her the man had probably been working for the Hollisters a long time.

All four children began to talk at once, but Tallulah managed to get their full attention. "Mr. Garroway is going to fix the tire. That means I expect all of you to sit still and quiet until he gets the job done. Then we can all go home."

With those instructions, she climbed back out of the vehicle and joined the cowboy, who was already placing the jack in a position to lift the disabled tire off the ground.

"Is there anything I can do to help?" she asked.

Without bothering to look in her direction, he said, "Thanks, but I can manage."

As Tallulah watched him pump the lever of the jack, she had no doubt the man could easily manage the task. His shoulders were broad and even though his arms were covered with denim fabric, she could see they were bulging with muscles.

Did a man get in such fit condition just from handling horses? Or was Jim Garroway a natural? As the questions drifted through her thoughts, her gaze seemed to take on a will of its own and continued to travel downward to where his thighs were straining against the worn denim.

"Nanny Tally, I'm hot," Abagail whined. "Can we get out?"

"I want out, too!" Billy wailed.

Thankfully, the children's complaints interrupted Tallulah's daydreaming and she gave herself a mental shake as she moved around to the side of SUV and stuck her head into the open window of the back door.

"Be patient, kids. It will only be a few more minutes. And when we get home we'll all have some lemonade," she promised.

"And cookies," Evelyn added. "I want snick-erdoodles."

"Yuk!" Andrew responded to his cousin's request. "I want the cowboy kind. With nuts and chocolate."

The kids began to argue about the cookies and Tallulah decided not to intervene. At least they weren't screaming at each other, or trying to climb out of their seats.

The high-pitched buzz of the power wrench caught her attention, and by the time she walked back to the front of the vehicle, Jim had already removed the lug bolts and was in the process of removing the tire and wheel.

Tossing it aside, he said, "That one is done for."

"I'm assuming the spare is under the vehicle," Tallulah told him. "Those things aren't always easy to take down."

He rose to his full height and directed a look at her. "You know about getting a spare down, do you?"

"Unfortunately, I've had a few flats over the years. And three-fourths of those I changed myself."

His expression said her remark had surprised him or he flat-out didn't believe she could change a tire. She could've told him that she and her brother had been forced to learn how to take care of themselves years ago.

"There weren't any Good Samaritans around to help?" he asked.

With a rueful smile, she shook her head. "Not on the road where I lived. It was out in the country and rarely traveled."

His gaze met hers, and Tallulah felt a strange little kick right between her breasts. What in heck was wrong with her? Too much sun?

"I see," he said. "Well, I'm going to do a little cheating today. I have a spare in the back of the truck that will fit the SUV good enough for you to limp home. Using it will save us both some time. And from the sounds of those kids, they're getting restless."

She laughed lightly as sounds of the chattering children grew a bit louder. "Andy is supposed to be telling the others a story. But it sounds like they're all trying to drown him out."

"Poor Andy." A faint smile curved his lips. "I'd better get that tire so you can get them home."

Nodding, Tallulah moved to one side and watched while he went about finishing the task.

After he'd put the tools and the ruined tire into the back of his truck, he walked over to where she stood.

"That should do it, Tallulah. I'll let Blake know that the SUV needs a new tire before it's driven again."

Impulsively, she reached for his hand and gave it a grateful squeeze. "Thanks for all your help, Jim. You've been a lifesaver."

Surprise flared in his eyes, and it dawned on her that the touch of her hand had caught him off guard. Was he not that accustomed to having a woman touch him? Even in a very casual way?

The questions hardly had time to flash through her mind before he eased his hand from hers and stepped back.

"All in a day's work, Tallulah," he said. "Drive safely."

"Always," she replied.

He gave her a thumbs-up, and then after a wave to the children, climbed into the work truck. It wasn't until he'd started the engine that Tallulah realized she was standing in the middle of the road, staring after him.

Hoping the man hadn't noticed she'd fallen into some sort of momentary trance, she hurriedly climbed into the SUV and buckled her seat belt.

"Okay, everyone can yell yippee now. We're on our way home!" she said to the children as she started the engine and raised the windows.

While the youngsters all yelled the word at once and clapped with glee, Tallulah put the vehicle in gear, then automatically glanced in the side mirror to make sure the road was clear.

Jim Garroway's truck was still sitting a few short feet behind her. Was he waiting for her to make the first move?

Unsure of his intentions, she lowered the driver's

window and leaned her head out in order to cast a questioning look at him. He aimed a forefinger in the direction of the ranch.

She waved that she understood and slowly drove forward. He promptly pulled in behind her, and for the next few miles, Tallulah tried not to notice he was back there. But that was hard to do when every minute or so, she caught herself glancing in the rearview mirror.

The wake of the SUV's dust partially obscured his truck, but she didn't need a clear view to remind her of the cowboy's image. It was already burned into her brain, and Tallulah realized her reaction to Jim's rugged good looks was very immature. True, he was one hot hunk of man, but she had no idea if he was married or involved with someone. For all she knew, he might be a husband and a father to a house full of kids.

She'd already suffered through a disastrous marriage. And she'd moved to Arizona to put all that behind her. More than anything she wanted to make a new life for herself. Pining after another man, one who'd most likely be all wrong for her, was not the way to accomplish her goal.

Once both vehicles reached ranch headquarters, Jim watched Tallulah brake the SUV to a stop near the west end of the three-story ranch house before he continued on to the work yard. At the side of a huge white barn with a red roof of corrugated iron, he braked the truck to a halt and headed toward the entrance to Blake Hollister's office.

In the past, Blake had used an old feed room in the cattle barn for his work space. But as Three Rivers Ranch had grown, and visits from cattle buyers had become more frequent, Maureen Hollister, the family matriarch, had insisted it was time for Blake to have a modern, up-to-date office. The man had finally given in to having a new office built, but he'd insisted it remain connected to the cattle barn.

When Jim entered the outer room, Flo, the ranch's one and only secretary, was at her desk with the receiver of a landline phone pressed to her ear. As soon as the sixtyish, redheaded woman glanced up to see Jim, she waved him on to the door that led into Blake's office.

After a short knock to announce himself, Jim stepped into the comfortably furnished room to see Blake was sitting at his desk and barking instructions into the phone. Tall and muscular with a head full of dark hair that was usually covered with a black Stetson, the eldest of the Hollister offspring had reached the age of forty this past year. However, due to his father Joel's untimely death, he'd served as the manager of the mega-sized ranch for more than a decade now. Blake was one of those guys that had much rather have his leg thrown over a horse, but duty and responsibility kept him mostly tied to the business end of the ranch. Jim admired the man for his loyalty along with countless other reasons.

Spotting Jim, Blake quickly ended the conversation and leaned casually back in a black executive chair. "Well, knock a board off the barn!" he joked. "It's been ages since you've been in here. I thought you'd forgotten how to find the cattle barn."

Jim gave him a lopsided grin. "Oh, I remember how to get here all right. It's just that your brother always keeps me too busy with the horses."

Blake chuckled knowingly. "You know Holt. He never has enough horses to suit him." He motioned for Jim to take a seat in front of the wide cherrywood desk. "What's going on over at the horse barn? Anything I should know about?"

Easing into the heavy wooden chair, Jim said, "Everything is good. Having Colt and Luke working with us has made a world of difference. Those two guys are the best."

Blake grinned and nodded. "Yeah. The Crawford brothers are a great asset to the ranch. So what about you? Everything going okay?"

Okay. Yeah, Jim thought, that was probably the best word to describe his life. It was good, but uneventful. He worked every day of the week from sunup to sundown and went home every night to a quiet, empty house. And because that was the way he wanted things to be, he couldn't complain.

"Sure. No problems."

"I'm glad to hear it." Blake rose from the chair and walked over to a small table with a coffee machine. "Want a cup? Sophia just brought down fresh cookies from the kitchen a few minutes ago."

"No, thanks, Blake. If I don't show up at the horse barn pretty soon, Holt's probably going to put out an APB for me. I got detained on the way home from town. That's why I stopped by to see you."

Blake filled a ceramic mug with coffee and carried it back to the desk. "What do you mean, detained? You got stopped by the law and handed a speeding ticket?"

Jim grunted with amusement. "Nothing like that. A few miles out from the ranch, I ran into your new nanny and the children. They were stranded on the side of the road with a blown tire on the SUV. I changed it with an old spare I had in my truck. But I thought you'd want to know the vehicle needs a new tire before it's driven again."

A concerned frown creased his face. "A blowout! Damn. Was everyone okay?"

"Everyone was fine. Ms. O'Brien had managed to get the vehicle safely to the side of the road. And the kids were all in their seats and behaving themselves."

Blake blew out a breath of relief. "Thank God

for that. I'm assuming they were coming home from the bus stop."

"Must have been. I followed them back to the house—to make sure there wasn't a problem with the spare."

Sinking into the desk chair, Blake said, "Thanks, Jim, for taking care of things. Glad you came by at the right time. I'm sure Tallulah was grateful for your help."

"Appeared to be," Jim said while recalling the way she grabbed his hand and squeezed it. She'd more than surprised him with that move. Come to think of it, just about everything about the woman had surprised him. Especially, the beautiful way she'd looked standing out in the middle of the road with her dark brown hair whipping around her pretty face. The smile she'd given him had been totally genuine and very unforgettable. "To tell you the truth, I had the feeling she wouldn't have been intimidated to change the tire herself."

Amused by Jim's suggestion, Blake said, "That's not surprising. Tallulah is a resourceful woman. Sometimes she cares for six or seven kids at the same time and handles the job with ease. Kat calls her an angel come to the rescue. And I have to agree. She's made life easier for all of us. And with our twins coming in a few months, I couldn't be happier that Tallulah is here. Kat needs all the help she can get and then some."

Blake was already father to teenage son, Nick, and four-year-old twins, Abagail and Andrew. Plus, this past December, during one of the Hollisters' Christmas parties, it was announced that Katherine was pregnant again. The news had surprised and delighted everyone. But the shocks hadn't ended there. A few days later, there'd been another stunning revelation, especially to Holt and Isabelle, who hadn't known at the time that she was also pregnant. Only six months earlier, Isabelle had given birth to their second son, Axel. Now, the horsewoman was expected to deliver their third child in June, while Katherine and Blake's second set of twins were due to arrive before summer's end.

Jim was happy for the whole Hollister family. But there were times he couldn't stop himself from wondering what-if. He couldn't stop the painful memories, or the awful longing for what might have been. But that part of his life was over, and he'd long ago decided it wasn't meant for him to be a family man.

Pulling his wandering thoughts back to the present, Jim said, "No doubt Tallulah will take a big load off Kat. But I wonder…"

After a long, awkward pause, Blake shot him a wry look.

"Let me guess," he said. "You're trying to figure out why a pretty young woman like her doesn't have a home and children of her own. Right?"

A wave of hot color crept up Jim's neck. "I… uh…something like that. Today was the first time I'd met her. She's not what I expected."

Actually, when he'd heard about Taggart's sister coming from Texas to care for the Hollister kids, he'd assumed she'd be a plain, middle-aged woman. Like an aunt he'd had as a child, who'd patted the top of his head and given him pieces of hard candy.

He couldn't have been more wrong, he thought, as the image of Tallulah in a pair of tight skinny jeans and a bright yellow tank top paraded through his mind. She wasn't one of those women with a stick straight figure. No, she'd been lushly curved in all the right places. And he'd had to work at not staring.

Blake chuckled. "What were you expecting? The stereotypical image of a stern old maid? Tag would get a laugh out of that."

His jaws still burning with color, Jim said, "No doubt."

"I'll tell you, Jim, Tag is thrilled to have his sister here on the ranch. He wasn't happy with the way her life was going back in Texas. Supposedly, she worked for a hard-nosed jerk. Plus, their father, Buck, was always trying to sponge off Tallulah. But that's a whole other story. And I shouldn't be repeating personal things about the O'Brien family."

Nor should Jim be listening, he thought. Tallulah O'Brien was none of his business. Even so, the tidbits of information Blake had just thrown at him had made him curious about her. That and the fact that she was the first woman he'd met in the past nine years who'd made him momentarily forget he was a widower.

Clearing his throat, he said, "Sounds like the move here was beneficial for her and your family."

Blake thoughtfully sipped his coffee. "You know, Jim, when things are going good, a guy needs to be thankful. Since Mom and Uncle Gil got married last year it seems like everything on the ranch and with the family has gotten better. The market for Three Rivers cattle is booming. Not to mention the high prices that Holt is getting now for the horses. We've had healthy babies born to the family and friends. And a few weddings and engagements have taken place. But I'll admit there are times I lay down at night and wonder what might suddenly crack."

Jim knew all too well what it was like for something in a person's life to suddenly crack. He'd endured it firsthand when he'd lost his wife and unborn child. But it wasn't like the Hollisters hadn't endured their fair share of miseries, either.

"Your father's death cast a shadow over your family and the ranch for a long while," Jim said with a shrug of his shoulders. "Things happen for a reason. But it's tough trying to figure out those reasons."

"When Dad was killed, Mom said the very same thing. For a long time I tried to figure the why of the tragedy. Now I've come to the conclusion that the why no longer matters. Clearly, Mom and Gil were meant to spend the rest of their lives together. And that's enough reckoning for me."

Was Blake hinting at the idea of there being a woman out there somewhere for Jim? One he was supposed to spend the rest of his life with? If so, he could've told the ranch manager that he wasn't about to let himself fall in love with another woman. As far as he was concerned, the emotional cost was too high.

Jim scooted to the edge of his seat. "I've sat here long enough," he announced. "I need to get on to the horse barn."

Blake's expression turned playful. "You haven't let my brother or any of the guys talk you into climbing on a bronc here lately, have you?"

Chuckling, Jim rose and walked to the door. "I'm not that crazy. I'll leave bronco busting to Holt and the Crawford brothers."

Giving him a thumbs-up gesture, Blake said, "See you, later, Jim. And thanks for helping Tallulah."

He gave the ranch manager a backhanded wave. "Anytime, Blake."

But as he left the office and headed to his truck, he hoped like hell he didn't run into Tallulah O'Brien anytime soon. She was the kind of woman who could wreck a man's peace of mind.

Chapter Two

Later that night, after helping Katherine and Roslyn get the children ready for dinner, Tallulah made her way to the kitchen, where she usually ate the evening meal with the Hollisters' house cooks, Reeva and her granddaughter, Sophia. Most nights Sophia's fiancé, Colt, joined the three women, but tonight the young horse trainer and Reeva were both absent from the warm kitchen.

"Don't tell me you're all by yourself," Tallulah said, as she walked over to where Sophia was filling a plate with baked chicken and various vegetables.

The petite brunette wrinkled her pretty nose. "Unfortunately. Colt is busy at the barn helping Holt with a mare. And Gran seemed extra tired this evening so I persuaded her to go home early and let me deal with the cleaning up."

Tallulah fetched a plate from the cabinet and rejoined Sophia at the industrial-sized cookstove. "I'm still amazed at how Reeva shows up long before daylight and cooks three meals a day. I only hope I can do half of what she does when I reach my early seventies. Actually, I'm not sure I could do half of what she does at the age I am now."

Sophia laughed softly. "Thirty years old? You're still a youngster." Her words were followed with a wistful sigh. "Sometimes I wish Gran would retire or, at least, chop her work hours down to half a day. But she'd be horrified at the idea. No, let me change that. She'd be downright angry."

"I wouldn't want to be the one to suggest a partial retirement. For the short time I've been here, I've already learned that Reeva can be rather fierce when she gets riled," Tallulah replied.

Sophia sighed again as she ladled seasoned rice onto her plate. "I'm not about to suggest any such thing to Gran. She'll have to be the one to figure out when she wants to slow down. I'm praying she'll have a few more years at her job. Because this kitchen and cooking for the Hollisters is her whole life. Take it away and she'd lose her purpose. That's when a person goes into a downward spiral. You know what I mean?"

"I do," Tallulah answered, as she dropped a helping of steamed asparagus onto her plate. "We all need something to make us feel useful and needed. Back in Muleshoe, a woman who was supposedly a friend suggested my weekend job at a day care in town was tacky. Even though it made me feel useful."

Sophia snorted. "What did she think when you took this job as nanny?"

"She suggested that I should want more out of life than taking care of someone else's kids. At first her remark made me angry. And then, like an idiot, I let it get to me. I started doubting my decision to make such a drastic change. But thankfully, my brother helped me realize I had to do what was best for me. Not what others thought I should do."

"When I moved here to the ranch and began cooking with Gran, my friends back in California gave me the same misguided advice. They all thought I was crazy for giving up a high paying job as an interior designer to stand over a hot stove all day for a bunch of tobacco chewing cowboys."

Tallulah laughed. "I don't think I've seen any of the ranch hands around here spitting tobacco."

"Like I said. They were misguided. In more ways than one."

Sophia's decision to make a change in her life had been far riskier than her own, Tallulah thought. But the gamble had obviously paid off. Now Sophia had a job she loved. A handsome horseman had slipped a beautiful engagement ring onto her finger, and the couple was planning a June wedding.

"Well, I didn't have an impressive job back in Muleshoe, by any means. But to some people an office job is more respectable than being a nanny."

The two women carried their plates over to a built-in booth situated a short distance down the same wall from the stove.

"Some people are fools," Sophia said, as the two women took a seat across from each other. "You're so important to the family—to all of us, really."

Tallulah cast a grateful glance at the younger woman. "That's kind of you to say. But honestly, once I got here and met the Hollister children, I knew I'd made the right choice." She laughed lightly. "Even when there are times I feel like I'm the ringleader of a circus."

Laughing with her, Sophia said, "The children were all excited this evening when you got them home from the bus stop. I guess having a tire blow-out was fun for them."

Tallulah stirred sugar into her iced tea. "They saw it as an adventure. Which was a good thing. And they didn't give me any problems."

Sophia's expression turned shrewd. "So what did you think about Jim?"

The question caught Tallulah completely off guard. "What do you mean?"

"Don't be coy," Sophia said with a suggestive grin. "Did you think he was cute?"

Cute? That was hardly the word to describe Jim

Garroway, she thought. "Isn't the man a little too old to be called cute?" Tallulah suggested.

Sophia frowned. "Old? The sun must have been in your eyes, Tallulah! I imagine Jim is in his thirties. Probably close to your brother's age."

Frowning, Tallulah forked up a piece of asparagus. "I didn't mean old in that context. The word cute is for—well, teenage boys or young men in their twenties. Jim is more of a—" She paused, embarrassed by what she'd been about to say.

Her eyes twinkling, Sophia prodded, "Go ahead, Tallulah, say what you're thinking."

"Okay," she conceded. "A hot hunk of man."

Sophia put down her fork long enough to clap her hands. "Yippee! You're finally thinking like a woman."

Amused, Tallulah shook her head. "I'm afraid to ask what that's supposed to mean."

"Like you don't know? This is the first time, since I've met you, that you've shown an inkling of interest in one of the single men here on the ranch."

Tallulah latched on to one important word. "Jim is single?"

Picking up her fork, Sophia said slyly, "He is."

"Do you know him personally?"

"Actually, I've spoken with Jim a few times when I've visited the horse barn. He works there with Colt and his brother, Luke. Colt has mentioned to me about Jim being single. He believes the man ought to find somebody to share his life with." A dreamy look spread across Sophia's face. "After Colt and I got engaged, he believes every guy should have a girl."

"Hmm. Well, speaking from experience—not every man needs a girl in his life. Some are very satisfied to be fancy free and do their own thing. I imagine Jim Garroway is that very type."

Sophia frowned. "Wouldn't it be better to find out for yourself what type he is? Instead of assuming?"

Would she? Ever since the man had climbed out of his truck and walked up to her, Tallulah had found it impossible to push his image from her mind. It was scary to think how a total stranger, a man she'd spent less than fifteen minutes with, could have such a strong effect on her.

"I don't want to invite trouble into my life," she replied to Sophia's question.

The woman rolled her eyes. "Why would Jim be trouble? He's a supergood guy, Tallulah. I'm sure he'd be a perfect gentleman."

"I doubt the Hollisters would have a man on their payroll who was anything less than a gentleman."

"If you believe that, then what's holding you back? I thought you told me that you've dated a bit since your divorce."

Tallulah pushed a bite of chicken from one side

of her plate to the other. "I have, but the dates were only casual. More like friends having dinner together, nothing—well, passionate."

"Playing it safe, huh? Nothing wrong with that. Until you start getting lonely for a man's arms around you."

Grimacing, Tallulah looked at her. "Look, Sophia. I moved here to Arizona to start over. Not to repeat the same mistakes I made with Shane. That means keeping a cool head."

"In other words, keep a safe distance from men." Sophia shook her head. "I made the same vow when I first moved here to the ranch. I'd gone through hell with Tristan and wasn't sure if I could ever let myself love or trust again. But I quickly learned that when the right person comes along everything in your life changes."

Since her move to Three Rivers, Tallulah had grown really close to Sophia and it touched her deeply to think how much the young woman wanted her to be happy and loved. But Sophia didn't understand that her broken marriage to Shane had shut off her emotions.

Yes, maybe she could look at Jim Garroway and feel a spark of physical attraction. A woman would have to be dead to glance at him and not feel a few sparks. But Tallulah wasn't sure she was ready to open the closed doors of her heart. Not even to a man with sky blue eyes and a charming grin that had sent tiny shivers up and down her spine.

"Yes, you've found your soul mate. You've been very blessed, Sophia. But where Jim is concerned, you're forgetting one major detail."

Sophia looked at her in surprise. "Oh, what's that?"

"Even if I was interested in him, he might not find me the least bit attractive."

A few seconds passed before Sophia burst out laughing. "Tallulah, that's the funniest thing I've heard in ages. Why, I bet right now Jim is thinking about you and kicking himself for not asking you for your phone number."

"Oh sure. I'm a femme fatale. And Jim didn't look like anybody's fool."

"He's nothing close to a fool. He's smart enough to know a good thing when he sees it."

Tallulah pointed at Sophia's plate. "Finish your dinner and I'll help you clean up the kitchen."

Sophia reached over and patted the top of Tallulah's hand. "I want you to be happy. That's all."

"Why wouldn't I be happy? I'm living here in the big house in a nice little upstairs suite of my own. Even better, I get to be with the children, the Hollisters, and all of you here on the ranch. I'm happier than I've been in years. Why spoil it with a man?"

Sophia rolled her eyes. "When you finally meet the right guy, you won't have to ask that question."

Tallulah didn't reply. The subject of love and the sexy wrangler was making her very uncomfortable.

Thankfully, Sophia must've decided to give her a break because she dropped the subject and began to talk about a pair of rescue cats Roslyn had brought from the Hollister Animal Hospital and given a home in one of the ranch's hay barns. But later, as Tallulah helped Sophia put away the leftovers and deal with the dirty dishes, she found herself thinking about Jim and, like a fool, wondering when she might have the chance to see him again.

The next afternoon, Tallulah had the children seated at the kitchen table for their after-school snack, when the phone located on the wall at the end of the cabinets rang.

Reeva, a tall, slender woman with a long, salt-and-pepper-colored braid hanging down her back, picked up the receiver.

"The kitchen," she answered, then after a pause said, "Yes, Tallulah's here. She's having coffee while the kids eat their snacks. You want to speak with her?"

The mention of her name had Tallulah glancing curiously over at the cook. No one called her on a house landline. It was much easier to contact her by cell phone.

After another long pause, Reeva said, "Okay. I'll give her the message. Better give her a few minutes, though. The kids haven't finished eating."

Reeva hung up the phone and walked over to the table.

"Who was that?" Tallulah asked.

Shaking her head, the cook muttered, "A man who's never had to corral a bunch of kids. Holt wants you to bring this bunch down to the horse barn."

The ranch yard was usually bustling with cowboys, along with all sorts of trucks, livestock trailers and haying equipment. Large holding pens were always full of cattle and horses. From the stories the children related to Tallulah, she knew they sometimes visited the ranch yard with their parents. But Tallulah hadn't yet taken the kids on such a trip.

"All of them?" Tallulah asked, while glancing at the housekeeper's two-year-old daughter, Madison. While the older children were home from school, the little girl stuck to them like glue. "Wonder if that means Madison, too?"

Reeva let out a short laugh. "Holt won't care if you bring four or ten kids. Jazelle is cleaning Maureen's office. I'll let her know you're taking Madison with you." The woman started toward the phone. "You do know where the horse barn is, don't you? It's the biggest building you'll see once you pass the cattle barn."

"Not long after I moved here Maureen took me on a tour of the ranch yard. I think I remember where most things are located," she told the cook, then asked, "Do you have any idea why he wants us at the horse barn?"

Reeva shrugged. "Something about a surprise for the kids. That's all I know."

By now, the children had picked up on the women's conversation. And all of them, including little Madison, were bouncing on their seats and shouting out questions.

Billy was the loudest. "I'm all finished eating, Nanny Tally. Can I go get my cowboy boots?"

"I want mine, too," Andrew said.

"Me go!" Madison yelled, while banging her spoon on the high-chair tray. "Me go see cows!"

Evelyn quickly chimed in. "I want my jeans."

"Yeah," Abby seconded her cousin's request. "We can't wear our dresses!"

Seeing the children were far too excited about the barn visit to finish their snacks, Tallulah said, "Okay. Everyone upstairs to change. But do it quickly. Your Uncle Holt is busy and we don't want to keep him waiting."

The four older kids jumped up from the table and raced out of the kitchen, while Tallulah hurriedly began to unstrap Madison and lift her from the high chair.

"Go! Go! Nanneee!" Madison screeched happily and hugged her arms tightly around Tallulah's neck.

Laughing, Tallulah kissed the girl's cheek. "Yes, you're going, too, Maddie. I'm not about to leave you behind."

From the opposite end of the kitchen, Sophia glanced away from the pot she was stirring and called out, "Don't bother with the table, Tallulah. I'll clean up the mess."

"Thanks, Sophia."

Carrying Madison on her hip, Tallulah hurried out of the kitchen and up the stairs to round up the rest of the group.

Five minutes later she was loading the children into the SUV that had been repaired with a new tire.

"Why can't we walk to the horse barn, Nanny Tally?" Andrew asked as Tallulah fastened the boy's seat belt across his lap.

"Yeah." Abagail seconded the query. "Mommy always walks with us. It's more fun."

"I promise, children, we'll all take a walk to the ranch yard in a few days. Right now, we don't want to keep your uncle waiting. And the quicker we get there, the sooner you'll see the surprise."

Billy suddenly yelled from his seat in the back.

"I know what it is. Daddy got us a goat! 'Cause he said we needed goat milk to make us strong. But I'm already strong. See?"

As Tallulah climbed into the driver's seat, she glanced in the rearview mirror long enough to see Billy attempting to make a muscle on his arm. The effort caused his sister to giggle loudly, and then the whole bunch was laughing and yelling out their own guesses as to what the surprise would be.

"Goats! Ride a goat, Nanneee!"

Madison's idea on the matter caused another loud uproar of laughter from the older kids, but Tallulah didn't try to quiet them. They were having too much fun. Besides, she was only half focused on the children's loud banter. She was remembering Sophia's remark about Jim working at the horse barn. If that was the case, then there was a chance that Tallulah might see the man again. And she wasn't sure how she felt about the possibility.

Quit lying to yourself, Tallulah. You know you're just itching to see the wrangler again. You went to sleep thinking about him and you woke up thinking about him.

"The horse barn is right up there, Nanny Tally. See? It's white, too. Like the cattle barn where Daddy works."

The sound of Abagail's direction pushed away the taunting voice inside Tallulah's head, and she forced her attention on the massive building on the right side of the roadway.

Two huge double doors were opened and laid back against the outside walls, while there was a smaller closed door just to the side of the wide entryway.

"Nanny Tally, stop here!" Andrew called out. "We go in the big doors."

"Yeah, they're open," Abagail declared the obvious. "We don't have to go through the little door."

Taking the children's advice, Tallulah parked near the side of the building in a spot she hoped would be out of the way of any passing work vehicles.

She was concentrating on unbuckling seat belts and helping the children to the ground when a male voice sounded behind her.

"Could you use some help?"

The deep timbre of the voice was vaguely familiar, and Tallulah's heart began to hammer with anticipation as she glanced over her shoulder to see Jim Garroway standing a few feet behind her.

Today his Western shirt was striped in various shades of green, while his blue jeans were covered with a pair of scarred and worn, butterscotch-colored chaps with a tooled belt and short fringe running along the outside length of the leg. With his dark brown cowboy hat angled low on his forehead, Tallulah could only think he looked very Western and all man.

"Oh. Hello, Jim."

"Hello." He moved closer to her and the children. "I saw you drive up and thought you might have your hands full."

Appreciating his thoughtfulness, Tallulah gave him a grateful smile. "You thought right. I've given the children orders not to leave my side. But they tend to get excited and forget orders."

He said, "Holt is at the back of the barn. Near the foaling area. I'll go along with you and make sure the kids don't get too distracted with the stalled horses."

"Thanks. I'd appreciate it. If you can handle the boys, I'll keep the girls with me," she told him, then reached inside the vehicle for Madison, who was beginning to whimper with fear of being left behind.

"It's okay, Maddie. I'm not about to forget you," she told the dimple-cheeked girl with a head full of blond curls.

As she closed the vehicle door behind her, she noticed Jim regarding Madison with curiosity.

"Is she your daughter?"

"Mine? Oh, no. I don't have any children," she told him. "This is Madison Murphy, Jazelle and Connor's little girl. I imagine you know them."

He glanced at the toddler before his gaze moved on to Tallulah's face. "I do. I'd just never met their daughter before."

Apparently, he wasn't a frequent visitor at the ranch house, she thought. Which explained why she'd never seen the man until yesterday.

"Well, Maddie wanted to come, too. But I think I'd better carry her." She moved a step closer to the rugged wrangler. "Say hello to Jim, Maddie."

Her blue eyes big and wide, the girl studied Jim for a moment and then giggled loudly and pointed a forefinger at him. "Jim ride goat! Yippee!"

Hearing her, the older kids started laughing, and Tallulah was glad to see Jim also chuckling at Madison's announcement.

"I'd probably do a better job at goat riding than horse handling," he said wryly, then reached for Andrew's and Billy's hands. "Come on, boys. Let's lead the way."

With Abagail and Evelyn walking close at her side and Madison in her arms, Tallulah followed Jim inside the cavernous building.

Although there were skylights in the roof high above their heads and fluorescent light fixtures hanging from the rafters, the interior was dim and shadowy, especially compared to the bright sunlight outside. The scents of alfalfa hay, horse manure and wood shavings immediately assaulted her nostrils, while nickering horses, whirring fans, the voices of the barn workers and the low volume of a radio all merged to create a cacophony of sounds that very nearly drowned out the excited shouts of the children.

"I've never seen inside this barn," Tallulah told Jim as the whole group walked down a wide dirt alleyway. "It's enormous. And there are so many horses. Beautiful horses."

"Three Rivers Ranch doesn't do anything in halves, Tallulah. Everything is first-rate. Although, I imagine you were picturing the barn to have a concrete floor and the stalls to be fancy."

"To be honest, I didn't know what to expect," she admitted. "This is more like an older, traditional type barn."

"You're right. The Hollisters are sticklers about doing everything they can in the simple, original way—the Western way. They take pride in that. But I'm sure your brother has probably already talked to you about how the ranch works and the way the Hollisters do things."

"He's talked to me about the cattle division," Tallulah admitted, "but not much about the horse division. It's all very different from the ranch where he worked back in Texas."

"Pony, Nannee! See? I wanta pet him!" Madison patted a hand against Tallulah's cheek to garner her attention, then pointed to a palomino horse that was hanging his head over a stall gate.

"We can't do that, Maddie," Tallulah told her. "The pony might bite."

"He very well would bite," Jim said to Tallulah. "He's a stallion. Biting is their nature."

Tallulah glanced over at him and wondered what it was about the man that made her heart thump just a bit faster. She'd been around cowboys all her life. She was used to seeing rugged men wearing jeans and boots and hats pulled low to shade their face. Even so, none of them had looked like Jim, she decided. His chiseled features and strong, lanky build reminded her of the images she'd seen in paintings done of the early West. Like a man who'd lived hard and fought hard to survive.

"Do you handle the stallion?" she asked, while thinking he probably approached the horse without an ounce of trepidation.

He looked at her with an expression that seemed a bit dry, but that was only a guess on her part. Just from her brief encounter with the man yesterday and now today, she'd decided he wasn't one to show much emotion. In fact, just by looking at him, it was impossible to tell what he was thinking."

"Uncle Jim, did Daddy get us a goat?" Evelyn suddenly spoke up.

Billy followed his sister's question with one of his own. "Does it have horns and milk?"

Before Jim could reply, Madison grabbed on to that one important word and happily shouted it next to Tallulah's ear.

"Goat! Ride a goat!"

"We're gonna get milk from the goat, Maddie. We're not gonna ride it!" Andrew corrected the little girl.

Over the heads of the children, Jim arched a questioning brow at Tallulah. "They think this visit to the barn is about a goat?"

Tallulah had to bite her lip to keep from laughing. "It's a subject they've been discussing. But I'm not sure Holt deals in goats."

For the first time since she'd met him, Jim laughed outright. The sound was deep and vibrant and acted on her senses like a warm hand sliding over her bare skin.

"Not yet, anyways," he said.

By now they'd reached the end of the alleyway where the stalls ended and a narrow pathway led between a wall and a large round pen equipped with a tall shower and a concrete floor.

"That's where the horses take a bath, Nanny Tally," Abagail informed her. "They get soap in their hair like Mommy puts in mine."

Tallulah smoothed a hand over the crown of Abagail's dark hair. "I'm sure it makes the horses' hair look as pretty as yours."

"I don't like baths," Andrew spoke up. "It's yukky to get wet. Unless we're swimming in the lake."

While Evelyn began to recite the merits of taking a bath or stinking, Tallulah glanced furtively at Jim. From what Sophia had told her, the man was single.

Which probably meant he didn't have children, either. But had he ever wanted a wife and children? Or was he content to live a solitary life? Either way, she told herself that Jim Garroway's feelings on the subject of having a family hardly mattered to her.

Their stroll through the barn continued until they reached a closed metal door painted a dull brown to match the cinder-block walls.

"Holt is in here in the foaling area," Jim said to Tallulah as he released his hold on the boys' hands long enough to open the door. "And in case you're worried about the kids seeing something upsetting, nothing is being born today."

"Thanks for being so thoughtful of the children," Tallulah told him.

A wan smile touched his lips. "Growing up on a ranch, they'll see plenty of births soon enough."

Nodding that she understood, she ushered the girls through the open doorway and Jim followed with the two boys.

"There's Uncle Holt!" Abagail instantly shouted as the tall cowboy strode toward the group.

Shortly after Tallulah arrived at Three Rivers, she'd met all four of the Hollister brothers. Blake managed the entire ranch, while Holt headed the horse division. Chandler, second to the oldest, was a veterinarian with a highly successful animal clinic on the outskirts of Wickenburg. Joseph, the youngest of the brothers, worked as a deputy for Yavapai County. All were successful, family-oriented men, although she'd heard stories that Holt had once been the wild playboy of the bunch. But after meeting Isabelle, he'd surrendered to love and marriage.

"Hey, kids!" he greeted, encompassing everyone with a smile. "Ready to see your surprise?"

They all shouted "yes" at once, making Holt laugh.

"I think I got the message," he said, then turned his attention to Tallulah. "Thanks for bringing the whole crew."

"No problem," she said, then gestured to Jim. "Jim helped me get the kids safely through the barn."

The rugged horseman turned a grin on Jim, who had a sheepish expression on his face. "No need for you to look so uncomfortable, Jim. The boys won't bite you. At least, I don't think they will."

Jim gave him a half-hearted smile. "I'm used to handling yearlings."

"Horses are about the only thing I've known of you handling," Holt said with a grunt of amusement, then moved over and plucked Madison from Tallulah's arms. "Come here, Maddie, and let me carry you. The rest of you follow me."

Surprisingly, the children didn't try to run ahead of the adults. They all stuck with Holt, until they reached a small corral made of iron pipe painted a pristine white.

Inside the pen was a brown Shetland pony with a shaggy golden mane and tail. As soon as the little horse realized he had company, he trotted over and attempted to stick his nose through the railing.

The children all squealed loudly and immediately began shouting questions at Holt. Tallulah was impressed to see the chaos didn't seem to bother him. Instead, he managed to raise his voice above the melee and catch their attention.

"Everyone be quiet and listen. This is Ranger Red. He's going to belong to all of you, so that means you're going to share him."

"He's not red!" Abagail sagely pointed out. "He's brown."

Holt looked at Tallulah and winked. "No. He's not red," he told Abagail. "But that's his name, anyway."

"Can we ride him now?" Andrew burst out with what he considered the most important issue.

"Not this evening," Holt explained. "Ranger Red just took a long ride to get here. And he's not acquainted with his new home or you kids yet. After a day or two, he'll get settled. Then we'll saddle him up and everyone can take a ride."

Madison patted Holt's cheek. "Ride goat! Me ride!"

Laughing, Holt explained to the little girl that Ranger Red was a pony, not a goat, then turned a wry look on Tallulah and Jim. "I've been telling Isabelle that I wouldn't know what to do with a baby girl. But, you know, I think if we end up having a daughter, I can figure it out."

"How is Isabelle doing?" Tallulah asked.

Holt's wife was a horse trainer and more than once Tallulah had overheard Maureen expressing concern about her daughter-in-law overworking herself.

"Other than trying to take care of too many things on the ranch, she's doing fine," Holt answered.

From the corner of her eye, Tallulah noticed a tight grimace had come over Jim's face. Did his odd reaction have anything to do with Isabelle? Or was he simply wishing she and the kids would end their visit and let him and Holt get back to work?

What difference does it make if the man smiles or frowns, Tallulah? You've been telling yourself you're not interested. So quit thinking and wondering about the man.

Holt turned back to the children, who were all absorbed with the new pony. While he patiently answered their endless questions, Tallulah defied the annoying voice in her head and stepped over to Jim's side.

"Looks like the pony is a big hit with the kids," she said.

Jim glanced at her, and she was relieved to see the frown had vanished from his face. "Maureen thought her grandchildren were old enough to learn about having a horse of their own and believes Holt is a much better teacher than her. That's why she handed the task over to him. And Holt definitely has the patience to teach them the responsibilities of owning a horse and riding it."

"I'm sure you'd have the patience to teach them, too."

Shrugging, he glanced away from her. "Not really. I have plenty of experience with horses. Not with kids."

Tallulah thought she heard a bit of a strain in his voice. As though his not being experienced with children was next to criminal.

She laughed softly. "Don't feel badly. I know quite a bit about kids but very little about horses. Sounds like we need to exchange information."

He looked at her, and Tallulah's breath nearly caught in her throat as his blue eyes locked on to hers.

"I'm not planning on having any kids."

Jolted, but undeterred by his comment, she said, "That's okay. I'm not planning on having any horses, either."

Her reply must've caught him off guard because for a moment he simply stared at her, and then he actually smiled. Not the halfway sort, but a full-blown one that exposed a row of white teeth.

"I guess I deserved that."

Shaking her head, she smiled at him, and as she did, it dawned on her that she'd like to spend more time with this man. And if she didn't act now, she might not have another chance to make that happen.

She cleared her throat, then said, "Actually, I'm thinking you deserve a bit of payment for coming to my rescue two days in a row."

"Not really."

"Yes. Really. You've been so nice about helping me here in the barn with the kids. And I'd like to do something for you. Do you like Mexican food?"

"Is there anyone who doesn't?" he joked, then said, "Sure. I eat it all the time."

"Great. So would you like to come by the house this evening and have supper with me? Reeva and Sophia always cook tons of extra food. You won't be taking away from anyone's plate. I can promise you that."

Surprise flickered in his eyes and then he said, "Nice of you to ask, Tallulah, but I wouldn't want to intrude."

She noticed his gaze drifting over to where Holt and the children were showering Ranger Red with loving attention. Apparently, he thought she'd be eating with the Hollisters.

"Oh, you wouldn't be intruding at all," she told him. "I always eat in the kitchen with Sophia and Reeva. And Colt joins us whenever he's not busy.

But if you'd feel more comfortable about it, you and I could eat out on the back patio. What do you say?"

A faint frown marked a line between his brow as though he was contemplating a life changing decision. Making Tallulah wonder what he thought having dinner with her might do to him. Warp his mind? Or bore him senseless? And then it dawned on her that he might have already had a date planned with some other woman. The idea wasn't a pleasant one.

"I'm sorry, Jim. I should have asked first. You might already have dinner plans with someone else."

His brows shot up until they completely disappeared beneath the brim of his hat. "I never have more than two plans for dinner. Eating with the boys in the bunkhouse or at home with my cat."

The relief that flooded through her made her wonder if she'd lost her mind. "And which plan did you have chosen for tonight?" she asked.

"My cat was winning out."

She slanted him another smile. "Then maybe your cat won't mind if you miss dining with him or her tonight."

He studied her for a few charged seconds before he finally shrugged. "She'll probably survive. So, thank you. I'll be there. What time?"

"Better make it a few minutes past seven. I always help Kat and Roslyn get the children ready for dinner."

"That's fine with me," he told her.

Joy spurted through her, and though she was filled with the urge to throw her arms around him and give him a fierce hug, she managed to hold her enthusiasm down to a wide smile.

"I'm glad," she murmured.

"Hey, Jim," Holt called out. "If you'll take Ranger Red to his outside stall, I'll help Tallulah get the children back through the barn."

"Sure thing," Jim told Holt, then darted a glance at Tallulah. "I'll see you later."

"I'm looking forward to it," she told him.

But a few minutes later, as she was driving her and the children back to the ranch house, Tallulah asked herself what she was doing.

Last night, she'd assured Sophia that she wasn't ready to get involved with a man. She'd insisted that she wasn't going to let herself get interested in Jim.

Now her whole body was humming with excitement at the thought of being alone with the man. Had she lost her senses? Or was her heart trying to tell her it was time for her to be a full-fledged woman again?

Chapter Three

Fortunately, Jim's shirt was only dusty from working in the outside training arena. After taking the shirt off and giving it a good shake, he pulled the garment back on, removed his chaps and spurs, and ran damp hands through his hair.

He didn't know why he was bothering with his appearance. Other than following the code of manners to be decent and clean at the dinner table, there was no need for him to spruce up for Tallulah's sake. This wasn't a date. They were going to eat a meal together. That's all.

As Jim drove to the main house and parked at a graveled area around back, he continued to tell himself that Tallulah's impromptu invitation was nothing special. And it certainly wasn't meant to be romantic, or even personal. This was her way of saying thank you. There was no need for his runaway thoughts to make any more of the invite.

Still, as he walked across the yard and onto a back porch where the door to the kitchen was located, he couldn't help but feel a little awkward and even more nervous.

He was lifting a hand to knock on the door, when it swung open. Tallulah stood on the threshold with a large tray cradled in her arms and a wide smile on her face.

"Hi, Jim! Your timing is perfect. I just now gathered up our meal. At least, I think I have everything."

He inclined his head toward the tray. "Can I carry that for you?"

"If you'd like." She handed the heavy tray to him and, after shutting the door behind her, joined him on the porch.

He noticed she was wearing the same yellow flowered sundress and tall brown cowboy boots she'd been wearing earlier at the barn. "I already have one of the tables on the patio ready. Come on and I'll show you."

Jim followed her to the huge covered patio where the Hollisters often gathered for evening drinks before dinner. The patio also served as a party area when some special occasion called for a celebration. Which was a fairly frequent occurrence on Three Rivers.

When they reached the patio, she directed him to a small wrought-iron table already set with plates, silverware, and glasses filled with crushed iced. In the middle was a fat, squatty candle in a holder made of red pottery.

The wick was already lit, the flame gently flickered in the breeze, and though Jim realized it was there to keep away the bugs, the sight of it caused a tiny alarm bell to ring in his head.

A candlelit dinner. Just him and her. That wasn't Jim's kind of thing. Not since his wife had died.

Don't be stupid, Jim. The woman lit a candle to avoid being attacked by mosquitoes. She's hardly trying to seduce you!

Shaking away the ridiculous thoughts in his head, Jim placed the tray on an empty space on the tabletop, then helped Tallulah into one of the chairs. While he settled himself into the seat across from her, she poured tea into their glasses.

"We're the only ones out here," Jim stated the obvious.

"Everyone is having dinner," she explained. "Sophia and Colt were going to join us. But since he cracked his collarbone yesterday Sophia is babying him with a special chair and a pillow behind his back—so he'll be more comfortable than sitting out here."

Jim let out a droll grunt and she slanted him a look of surprise.

"You find something funny about Colt having a cracked collarbone?"

Not bothering to hide his amusement, he said, "Nothing funny about the cracked collarbone. I was with Colt when he got hurt. One of the two-year-old horses dumped him into a board fence."

She regarded him with disbelief. "And you laughed?"

"No. For a minute or two I was afraid he'd broken his neck. I'm the one who hauled him into the clinic to see a doctor and get it x-rayed. What I find amusing is that Sophia is babying him. Doesn't she realize that he's been riding horses all day today? The man is as tough as rawhide. He doesn't need a special chair. But I'm sure he's enjoying being fussed over."

Tallulah frowned. "Surely a doctor didn't advise him to keep riding."

"Ha! I doubt there's a hand on this ranch who'd follow a doctor's advice. That's not the cowboy way."

With a good-humored smirk, she said, "You sound like Tag. Even if my brother was delirious with fever or had both legs broken, he'd try to drag himself out to his horse. I should've realized Colt was just like the rest of you."

She pulled the linen cover from the tray and gestured for him to dig in. "Help yourself, Jim. I hope there's something here that you like. And there's plenty more in the kitchen, so no need for you to eat sparingly."

Hesitating, he said, "My mom always taught me that ladies should go first. You go ahead."

"Okay. I won't be bashful. To tell you the truth, I'm very hungry. It's been a busy day. I think my lunch consisted of three cheese crackers. That's been too long ago to remember."

Jim watched her ladle two enchiladas onto her plate, then a pair of beef-filled tacos. She had nice, smooth hands with short nails that were painted a shell pink. There were no rings on any of her fingers, including the most important one.

Her life was going nowhere back in Texas.

Blake's comments about Tallulah suddenly drifted through his thoughts. Had this lovely woman been married before, or engaged? If so, he couldn't imagine a man letting her go. And Blake had also made that remark about Tallulah and Taggart's father.

I think their father was always trying to sponge off Tallulah.

What in hell kind of man sponged off his own daughter? The sorriest kind, he grimly answered himself.

"I brought pico de gallo, too. And avocado slices." After opening a pair of small plastic containers, she spooned contents from both onto her plate, then pushed the small canisters toward him. "Help yourself. I'm finished."

"This is nice," Jim said as he filled his plate and the delicious smells of the food wafted up to his nostrils. "I think the cook in the bunkhouse was making goulash and cornbread for the crew. It's good. But not as good as this."

She lifted one of the tacos from her plate. "Do you eat with the bunkhouse cowboys as much as you do at home with your cat?"

"Probably an equal amount. I'm not a very good cook. I tend to burn things."

She chuckled, then bit off a mouthful of taco. After she'd swallowed it, she asked, "Since you don't live in the bunkhouse, do you have a house of your own here on the ranch?"

He shook his head. "My place isn't on Three Rivers property. But it's not far from here. Do you know where Sam and Gabby Leman live? The little house on past the Bar X entrance?"

"Yes. I know the place. That is, if you're talking about the Bar X foreman? He and Gabby are Holt's in-laws, right?"

Jim nodded. "Right on both counts. Well, not long after you pass Sam's house, there's a road that turns left and goes for only a short distance. My house is there. Next to a bluff and a grove of pines."

"Mmm. Sounds nice. Have you lived there for a long time?"

He spooned some of the pico onto his enchiladas. "Going on ten years. Ever since I went to work for the Hollisters. Before that I worked at Yavapai Downs. That's a horse racing track in Prescott Valley. Actually, it's been renamed to Prescott Downs now. I forget and still call it Yavapai."

Her brows arched upward. "What did you do there?"

"I was a groom. Feeding, grooming, bathing, walking the horses. The list goes on and on. That includes keeping them happy and content and making note of any little health issues."

"Sounds very involved," she said.

"It is," he replied. "You become the horses' closest companion."

"Did you like the job?" she asked, then explained, "I'm curious as to why you changed one horse job for another."

His gaze dropped to his plate, and for a moment he considered telling her he wanted to change the subject. But that would not only make him look small; it would probably make her feel very awkward.

"I liked the job. It was exciting. Especially when a horse I was closely connected with won a race. But while I was there…" Pausing, he had to draw in a deep breath before he could push out the rest of his words. "My wife died in an accident and afterward I—well, I needed a change. To make a totally different life for myself. Hiring on here was an answered prayer. Meeting the Hollisters and working on Three Rivers helped keep me afloat. Both mentally and financially."

She looked at him, and as her soft brown eyes slowly roamed his face, he greatly feared that she might start plying him with questions about his wife and how she'd died. He didn't want to go into that dark period of his life right now. Not because it was a secret, but because he didn't want this short time with Tallulah to end up a gloom fest.

Finally, she said, "I'm a little lost for words. Because I…would've never guessed the two of us have so much in common. I mean, I'm not a widow. But I was married for three years and it ended up not working out." Smiling wanly, she shook her head. "I stuck around in Muleshoe because I'd lived in the area for a long time and my friends and job were there. But Tag kept urging me to move out here to Three Rivers and he finally convinced me that I needed a change and to start over."

Jim stared at her, while an odd mixture of thoughts and emotions rushed straight at him. He'd been holding his breath, hoping she wouldn't question him about his late wife. But instead of pumping him for information, she'd shared some of her own. And now, damn it, he very much wanted to hear about her ex and why they'd not made a go of it.

"That's nice—uh, that you were given the chance to move here to the ranch. Are you living with your brother and his wife?"

"Oh no. Tag and Emily-Ann are still basically newlyweds with a baby. I wouldn't intrude on him and his family, even though they did offer for me to move in with them." She shook her head as she shoveled up a forkful of enchilada. "I live here in the main ranch house with the Hollisters. Before I arrived, Maureen had a couple of upstairs bedrooms turned into a little suite for me. It's very comfortable and has everything I need. Plus I'm right in the house in case I'm needed at odd hours of the night."

So she lived in the ranch house with the Hollisters. The fact didn't exactly surprise him. After all, she'd been hired as the family nanny, a very personal job. Obviously, Maureen and the rest of the Hollisters had put great trust in her.

"How do you like this area?"

She flashed a wide smile at him, and Jim was struck by the vibrant sparkle in her eyes. Whatever she'd left behind in Texas didn't appear to have followed her. At least, not tonight. She seemed happy and full of life, and in spite of himself, he felt her attitude lifting his mood.

"I love how different the land around here is. We're surrounded by mountains, but there's also desert terrain. But it's all the valleys of grazing land that have surprised me the most. I honestly wasn't expecting so much green out here."

"We have to use the water supply wisely. As for the prickly vegetation we have plenty of it," he said. "Makes for tough riding when the cowboys have to gather cattle from the chaparral. I'm sure Tag has told you how the men and the horses get scratched and stabbed with thorns."

She chuckled. "When I started talking about the beauty of the cacti, he told me all about getting the needles dug out of the men and the horses. I guess everything has its good and bad sides. Actually, I'm looking forward to what the winter months are like around here. I'm not a fan of cold weather, so I'm hoping I won't have to bundle up all that much."

"Our winters are usually mild," he said. "We don't get snow like they do in the northern part of the state."

"Living on the Texas plains, I've seen a few blizzards. They're horrendous on the cattle. Not to mention everything else." She glanced over at him. "Do you ever work with the cattle?"

"Once in a while I go on fall roundup. Just because I enjoy it. The Hollisters do roundup the old-fashioned way. Sleeping on the ground around the campfire and eating off the chuck wagon. But other than that week or so, Holt keeps me too busy with the horses to give me any time do much else. Every year the horse division has grown larger and larger."

She sipped her tea and Jim's eyes were drawn to her wet lips. Earlier, before they'd started eating, she'd been wearing a touch of coral lipstick. But now the food and drink had taken that away and he could see her bare lips were naturally a dusky pink color. He figured after a few hot kisses they'd turn an even deeper shade of rose.

Kisses? Hell, what was he doing thinking about kisses? Especially with this woman? He didn't know for certain, but she seemed like the family sort to him. The kind that wanted only one man. A man who'd be steady and loyal and capable of giving her everything she needed and wanted.

Leveling a pointed look at him, she said, "I have a feeling you're just as proud of that fact as Holt and his family."

The idea that she could already see or understand his feelings toward his job, and the ranch, took him by surprise. "I'm probably prouder," he murmured, then shrugged. "I guess you can tell my job is my life. And you're probably thinking that's not a good thing."

"On the contrary. It tells me that you were smart enough to choose to do something for a living that you love. I wish I'd followed your way of thinking. I stayed with a job that made me anxious and miserable for far too long."

He couldn't believe how curious he was about her. Ever since his wife had died, women had been little more than a passing thought to him. Oh, there'd been a few he'd found attractive, and for a while in those initial years after Lyndsey had died, he'd even forced himself to go out on dates. None of them had sparked his interest. So why was he so interested in Tallulah? Why did he want to ask her question after question?

"Your job was in Muleshoe? Or did you commute to a larger town?"

She chewed a bite of taco, then dabbed her lips with a napkin before answering. "Commuting was not for me. The only cities within driving distance were Lubbock to the south and Amarillo to the north. And both were over an hour's drive one way. No. I worked for a privately owned real estate office in Muleshoe. I did most of the paperwork to be sent to the title company. You know, all that boring legal jargon, survey calculations and section numbers—that sort of thing."

"Hmm. In other words, it was mentally stressful," he commented.

She rolled her eyes and then laughed. "Thank God I can laugh about it now. Back then, there wasn't a day went by that I didn't have to bite my lip to keep from telling my boss to go jump into a lake—of fire, preferably. He might as well have had a horsewhip or cattle prod in his office. He didn't know how to speak in a normal tone, especially if he was angry. Which was quite often. The customers in the doughnut shop next to us could hear his rants all the way through the walls of the building."

Frowning, Jim tried to imagine working under those conditions. He certainly couldn't have endured one day of it, much less years. "Were you the only employee?"

"There were three other women along with me. To tell you the truth, after a while, we mostly ignored our boss's tantrums. It was the only way to deal with the situation."

"So how did you go from working in a real estate office to a childcare job? The two have nothing in common."

She nodded in agreement. "Nothing at all. I worked on weekends at a day care in town. Plus friends often hired me to watch their children whenever they needed a babysitter. I've been doing childcare for a long time."

She obviously loved children, which made Jim wonder why she'd not had any of her own. True, she'd admitted her marriage had only lasted a short three years, but that was more than enough time to produce a child. Perhaps her ex-husband hadn't been keen on the idea, he thought. With Tallulah, he could see where that would've caused major problems.

"Sounds like you're experienced in dealing with kids."

His comment clearly amused her. "I'm not sure anyone can ever know all they need to know about caring for a child. Each one is different. And complex. Maybe that's the reason I like the job so much. It's a challenge."

"Well, it's a cinch you'll get plenty of experience around here," he told her.

Her laugh was soft and full of warmth. "Yes, and I'll be getting even more experience when Katherine delivers her and Blake's twins. Having two infants in the house is really going to keep me on my toes. But it's not really as bad as it sounds. As soon as Roslyn and Katherine get home from work in the evenings they take over caring for the children. Sometimes I help with their nightly baths and getting them to the dinner table, but that's only because I want to."

Babies and children. No matter where he went on the ranch, or how much he tried to avoid the subject, it seemed to follow him like a haunting shadow.

Hoping she couldn't detect a strain in his voice, he said, "I imagine you already know that Holt and Isabelle are expecting another child. Holt says it should arrive somewhere around the middle of June."

Nodding, she smiled. "Yes, I've visited with Isabelle a few times. She's such a fun person. And I'm amazed at how she manages to handle the children, plus all the work she does on her and Holt's ranch, the Blue Stallion."

Even though this latest pregnancy had been a surprise, Holt was delirious with joy over the prospect of becoming a father for the third time. Jim was happy for him. Actually, he was happy for Blake, too. And all the other men on the ranch, who'd been blessed with children. But that didn't mean he'd stopped feeling the loss of his own child. Or that he'd quit wondering why his family had been taken away from him.

"Do you ever take care of Holt and Isabelle's two boys?"

"Not on my own. But so far they've only been over here to the ranch a few times. Carter and Axel are both adorable. They're no problem. But it does get a bit hectic when Joe and Tessa bring their three children over. But that doesn't happen on a regular basis and when it does, Jazelle stays over to help me. And Nick, Blake's teenage son, is a real trooper about pitching in and helping with the kids. I can only hope that if I ever have a son of my own, he grows up to be as thoughtful and responsible as Nick."

If I ever have a son of my own.

In spite of the long years that had passed, memories of his son were still so raw and vivid he could hardly bear to let himself revisit the short, bittersweet moments he'd had with his child.

Cody Lynn Garroway had lived only six and a half days after his mother had died. At seven months gestation, his premature body had been perfectly formed and under normal circumstances he could have survived. But the accident that had taken his mother's life had caused too much trauma to his tiny body. Now, Jim could only guess as to what kind of son little Cody would've grown into.

"Jim? Is anything wrong?"

The haunting sounds of a beeping heart monitor and the voices of the pediatric nurses as they'd tended to his son were suddenly interrupted by Tallulah's point-blank question.

He blinked his eyes and gave himself a hard mental shake before he finally focused his gaze on her. Damn it, how long had he been staring off in space? Judging by the anxious frown on her face, he'd been unresponsive far too long.

"Wrong? Uh…no. I was thinking… I just remembered something I need to do at the house. Before it gets…uh…dark." The urgent need to escape had him putting down his fork and pushing back his plate. "I'm sorry, Tallulah. I really need to go."

Grabbing his hat from under his chair, he stood

and levered the battered felt onto his head. All the while, he sensed she was staring at him, yet he couldn't bring his gaze meet hers.

"Now?" she asked. "Reeva baked apple crumb pie."

The disappointment in her voice surprised him. He wasn't expecting that from her. Nor had he expected to feel regret for causing it.

Clearing his throat, he managed to reply, "I'll… uh…take a rain check on dessert, Tallulah. Thank you for the dinner. It was nice."

The feeling of being suffocated was rapidly consuming him, along with the need to escape, but as he turned to walk away, she jumped up and hurried around the table to intercept him.

Once she reached his side, she placed a hand on his forearm and Jim was glad the fabric of his shirtsleeve acted as a barrier, otherwise he figured his skin would've been scorched.

"I really wish you could stay longer, Jim. But if you're sure about needing to go, then I'll walk with you to your truck."

He realized he should ease his arm away from her touch, but he didn't want to appear standoffish. Nor could he resist the warmth radiating from her fingers.

"That isn't necessary," he told her.

"Nonsense. You're my guest. I want to see you off."

He darted a glance at her. "I'm not much of a guest, Tallulah."

"I'll be the judge of that."

He couldn't come up with one word to counter her remark, and when he failed to speak, she moved even closer and wrapped her arm around his.

Instead of walking off the patio, as he'd first intended, he stared at her in stunned confusion. But she merely smiled and urged him off the patio.

Jim couldn't remember the last time a woman had walked along beside him or touched him in such a way. Strangely enough, her presence reminded him that no matter the past, he was still a man. With a man's basic reactions to a female body. Just one more reason he needed to get home.

By the time they reached his truck, twilight had fallen and he hoped the shadows would hide the distress that was surely on his face. He didn't want this woman to ever guess he was a half-broken man.

Drawing in a deep breath, he said, "Goodbye, Tallulah. Maybe we'll run into each other again—sometime."

"Sometime?" Her brows arched faintly upward.

She sounded disappointed, but in his frame of mind, he could be misreading her. And anyway, what did it matter? he asked himself. He was hardly the kind of man she needed to start her life over.

Focusing his gaze on the toes of his boots, he said, "Well, the ranch is a big place. And the two of us have busy jobs."

"Yes, we do. But I hope we have a chance to get together again—soon. Maybe next time you can stay for dessert."

He looked up to see she was smiling at him, and for a split-second Jim wondered if this was how a man behaved once he'd lost his mind. Tallulah was a lovely woman. Any sane man would be looking for all kinds of excuses to spend time with her. But he couldn't think like a normal man. Not when the dark memories were tearing holes right through him.

"Yeah, maybe." He tried to smile, but his lips felt frozen to a stiff line.

"Yeah, surely," she said.

And then to his amazement, she stood on the tips of her toes and planted a kiss in the middle of his cheek.

"Thank you, Jim," she said softly. "Good night."

"Good night," he murmured and then hurriedly climbed into his truck and drove away.

With Jim's taillights in the distance, Tallulah walked thoughtfully back to the table on the patio and automatically began to scrape the scraps from Jim's plate onto hers.

She couldn't think of one thing she'd said or

done to make him jump up and hurry off. But for all she knew he might be the type of guy whose mood changed with the wind. Nice and attentive one moment, aloof and preoccupied the next. Still, she couldn't help but feel deflated by his sudden departure.

She was trying to tell herself not to give the whole incident a second thought, when Sophia appeared on the patio carrying a tray with a whole pie, a container of whipped cream and two dessert plates.

"Desert time," she cheerfully announced.

Tallulah refrained from groaning out loud. "I'm sorry you went to the trouble to bring the pie out here. Jim has already left for home."

Sophia looked incredulous. "Home? Are you kidding?"

Shrugging, Tallulah did her best to appear indifferent to the matter. "No joke. He left a few moments ago. He needed to do something at home. Or that's what he said, anyway."

Sophia frowned. "Must've been something urgent."

Until this very moment, she hadn't realized she'd had such a tight hold on her emotions. But now the reins she'd been gripping snapped, allowing a stampede of humiliation to trample all over her.

"I'm guessing his cat must've had a hangnail,"

she said drolly. "Or he instantly remembered he'd left the porch light on early this morning."

Sophia placed the dessert tray on the corner of the table and folded her arms against her chest. "What happened?"

Tallulah wished she knew the answer. "I'm clueless, Sophia. We were having a nice meal together—until he suddenly grabbed his hat and said he needed to leave. He jumped up like a wasp had stung him. I walked him to his truck and suggested we have dinner together again sometime. But he didn't make any promises. And the next thing I knew, he was climbing into his truck and driving away."

"How strange. Jim has always seemed like a laid-back kind of guy to me. In fact, Colt said if a firecracker exploded at Jim's feet, he doubted it would shake the guy."

"Obviously there's a side of Jim that you and Colt haven't seen before. I just happened to bring it out of him tonight."

The two of them had been talking so easily, Tallulah thought. Then seemingly out of the blue, his face had gone drawn and pale.

"We're making too much out of this," Tallulah said as she tried to ward off a heavy dose of rejection. "Jim simply realized I wasn't somebody he wanted to be around."

"And he needed to make a fast exit to get away

from you?" Sophia rolled her eyes. "Don't be silly. He got cold feet and ran scared."

Tallulah frowned. "I didn't do or say anything that might scare him off. It was only a friendly meal. I wasn't putting moves on him!"

Tapping a forefinger thoughtfully against her chin, Sophia said, "No. But he might have been putting moves on you—in his mind, that is. And that scared him."

Sophia's suggestion caused Tallulah to let out a short, incredulous laugh. If any kind of romantic thoughts about her had been going through Jim's mind, he'd kept them carefully hidden. Throughout the whole meal, she'd not detected a flicker of attraction on his face.

"No way! The two of us were talking about Kat and Blake's twins coming soon, and he mentioned Isabelle's pregnancy and how all the babies were going to give me plenty of experience. I talked about Nick helping me with the little ones whenever he was around and that's it. So see? There was nothing provocative or romantic about our conversation."

Sophia's brows arched with speculation. "Hmm. Jim doesn't have children. He doesn't even have a girlfriend."

Tallulah held back a sigh. Not for anything did she want Sophia to guess how much Jim's unexplained departure had affected her.

"Don't give it a second thought, Sophia. Actually, it's probably for the best. He's not…my type. And I'm clearly not his."

Sophia scowled at her. "How do you know you're not each other's type?"

In truth, during most of the meal, Tallulah had been thinking how much she was enjoying Jim's company and how so many things about him were the very things she admired in a man.

Tallulah deliberately avoided making eye contact with Sophia. "Well, we don't have much in common," she answered. "His thing is horses and mine is kids. They don't really mix."

"Ha! Tell that to the Hollister children. They're all horse crazy."

Tallulah gathered the last of the unfinished meal onto the tray. "You know what I mean, Sophia. I don't know much about his job, and he isn't all that interested in mine."

Sophia laughed off Tallulah's reasoning. "Colt doesn't know anything about cooking, either. And my knowledge about horses is minuscule, but neither of those things matter when we're together."

The dreamy note that slipped into Sophia's voice reminded Tallulah just how long it had been since she'd wanted to be in a man's arms.

She forced herself to meet Sophia's skeptical gaze.

"Yes, but it helps to have a few things in common. Anyway, it's not like I was expecting anything monumental to come out this little meal. So there's nothing wrong. I'm fine."

Sophia studied her for a moment, then with a commiserating groan, slipped an arm around the back of her shoulders. "Don't fib. I can see that you're disappointed. Right?"

Tallulah let out a resigned sigh. "Okay. I am somewhat disappointed. He's a nice man, and I guess I was hoping that he might find me interesting enough to want to ask me out—or something. And I don't know why in heck I was letting myself hope for that much. I'm much better off not dating at all. Just look what one little meal with a cowboy has done to me. I feel as deflated as that flat tire Jim took off the SUV yesterday."

Sophia gave her shoulder an encouraging shake. "Come on. You need a sugar buzz. Let's go in and dig into the pie."

Forcing herself to smile, Tallulah picked up the tray of leftovers and followed her friend into the house.

By the time Jim got home, took a shower and headed to the kitchen to make a pot of coffee, he was cursing himself and wishing someone was around to give him a hard kick in the seat of his pants.

He'd acted like a complete fool with Tallulah,

and right about now she was probably thinking she'd walk an extra mile just to avoid being anywhere near him. And he couldn't blame her. She'd been friendly and warm, and he'd repaid her by running off as though being with her had left him half-sick.

Groaning inwardly, he raked a hand through his damp hair and tried to push the whole incident out of his mind. But even as he put the coffee makings together and watched the hot brew drip into the carafe, he couldn't help but feel as though he'd lost out on something important tonight.

Hell, Jim, what could be so important about Tallulah O'Brien? The Hollisters' nanny is nothing to you. She never will be. So forget about the way she'd looked at you when she'd said goodnight. Maybe she had looked sweet and inviting. But you're not in the market for romance.

Closing his eyes, Jim pinched the bridge of his nose and tried to shake away the image of her warm lips curving upward, the twinkle in her brown eyes whenever she'd smiled at him. And that kiss she'd placed on his cheek had sent a jolt through the top of his head all the way to the soles of his boots.

Yes, he'd lost something all right, he thought ruefully. Tallulah might have given him the chance to become a whole man again.

Hell, what made him think she could change

his life? Or fix whatever was broken inside him? The idea was stupid. Since Lyndsey's death, he'd tried dating a few women. He'd even tried to make love to some of them. But he'd ended up merely going through the motions of the sex act. Without the deep connection of love, the outings had done nothing but make him miss his late wife even more. Each miserable encounter had convinced him that a man had only one chance at real love in his lifetime. And he'd lost his.

Wiping a weary hand over his face, he filled a mug with coffee, then grabbed a carton of half-and-half from the refrigerator. As he poured a hefty amount of milk and cream into the steaming liquid, he felt Georgette, his orange tabby, weaving back and forth between his legs.

"What are you doing in here? You've already had your supper," he reminded the cat.

Georgette's big green eyes stared up at him before she let out a plaintive meow that said supper hadn't been enough.

Shaking his head, Jim walked over to the cat's food bowl sitting at the end of a cabinet and dropped in a few treats. Georgette trotted over and began to eat with appreciation.

"You better enjoy those, young lady," Jim told the feline. "'Cause that's all you're getting for the rest of the night. Remember what the vet said about your weight? It's too much. And if you weigh more the next time he sees you, the blame will be on me."

Ignoring her master's words of warning, the cat continued to nibble the treats. Jim carried his coffee out to the living and sank into a large, overstuffed armchair.

A remote was located on a small end table located next to the left arm of the chair, but Jim didn't bother turning on the TV. Nor did he switch on a lamp. The darkness of the room allowed him to see beyond the wide picture window where intervals of rocky bluffs and piney foothills made up a mountainous vista that stretched endlessly toward the north.

Across the cozy room, on a fireplace mantel made of native rock, a photo of Lyndsey sat facing the window. Jim had placed the photo there nine years ago, when he'd first moved into the house. It had been his way of sharing the view with her. Which was a macabre idea, he supposed. But over these past years, he'd learned that a man who'd lost the most important things in his life didn't always think with common sense. And he'd do most anything, weird or not, to make the darkness inside him a little less bleak.

He was certain she would've loved this place he called home. During their four years of marriage, the two of them had lived in a rental. With its drafty windows, thin walls and worn flooring, the tiny house hadn't been much more than decent shelter. They'd often talked about the day they'd have the chance to move to something better.

To this day, not being able to give Lyndsey her dream home continued to haunt Jim. He'd wanted to give her so much. But he and Lyndsey had both come from humble beginnings, and money for anything more than groceries and utilities had been hard to come by. He'd not begun to get ahead and build financial security for himself until he'd moved here to Three Rivers Ranch.

I live here in the main ranch house with the Hollisters.

Tallulah's revelation meant two things. Her duties as a nanny didn't begin or end at a certain time of the day. And she didn't need a man to provide her with a home.

But she might need a man for other reasons, he thought. Like companionship. And love. And sex.

Did those reasons have anything to do with her dinner invitation? With the kiss she'd placed on his cheek?

He was telling himself not to be stupid when Georgette leaped into his lap, then climbed up his chest and rubbed her cheek against his.

"Aww, pretty girl, you don't have to tell me you get lonely. I know you do," he crooned, while stroking a hand down her back. "If I wasn't so selfish, I'd take you back to the horse barn where you can be with the other cats."

But Georgette had been with him since she was a very small kitten. Jim would miss the cat something awful if she wasn't here to see him off in the mornings, or greet him when he returned home at night.

Scratching the cat between the ears, he said, "But we could get you a cat friend. You can make each other happy. That's the way things should be. With cats. And humans."

The tips of his fingers touched the spot where Tallulah's lips had pressed against his cheek and the memory of that one brief moment saddled his heart with regret.

Even if Jim could manage to put the past behind him, Tallulah had already gone through enough problems in her life. She didn't need him and his baggage. He'd only bring her more problems.

Chapter Four

Nanny Tally, do we have to go to school tomorrow?"

From her seat on the corner of the children's large sandpile, Tallulah glanced over to where Abagail, Andrew and Madison were all happily digging with plastic shovels and pails. A few steps away on a stretch of green grass, Evelyn was trying to pull Billy in a little red wagon equipped with sideboards.

"Tomorrow is Saturday," Tallulah answered the girl. "That means you don't go to Kindergarten or pre-school."

"Yay! Yay!" Andrew shouted. "I want to ride Ranger Red all day long!"

"You're mean, Andy!" Abagail scolded her twin brother. "You'd kill Ranger Red if you rode him for that long."

Andrew stuck his tongue out at his sister and Madison was quick to imitate the boy. So much for teaching the child nice manners, Tallulah thought dryly.

"Andy do not stick out your tongue. Not at your sister or anyone," Tallulah said, gently reprimanding the boy, then turned to his sister. "And Abby, I don't believe Andy will ride Ranger Red long enough to hurt him. Your Uncle Holt will see to that."

"Ride Red!" Madison squealed. "Me ride, too!"

"Who says, you little monkey!"

At the sound of Jazelle's voice, the toddler glanced around to see her mother had walked up. The sight of the pretty blonde caused the girl to let out another happy screech.

"Mommy! Mommy!"

Laughing, Jazelle picked up her daughter and swung her onto her hip.

"Looks like you have the bunch under control," Jazelle joked. "No one is crying or pulling hair."

"Not yet," Tallulah said with a little laugh. "Did you come to get Madison? She's having a good time."

"Oh, I didn't come to get her. I'm taking a little break before I do more cleaning in the den. I only came out here to pass along a bit of news."

Tallulah looked at the housekeeper with interest. "What kind of news? Maureen is planning another party?"

Jazelle laughed. "Not yet anyway. But I'm expecting she'll come up with something soon." The smile on her face faded. "No. This isn't exactly fun news. Sophia just told me that Colt had to take Jim to the emergency room to get stitched up. Apparently, Jim lost quite a bit of blood."

Aghast at the thought, Tallulah stared at her. "What happened? Is he okay?"

Jazelle shook her head. "I'm not sure what happened. Something about a horse's shoe being loose and Jim was in the process of taking it off. He cut his hand pretty bad. The doctor says he'll be fine. Just not on full duty for a few days."

Relief poured through her. "I'm sorry the accident happened, but glad he'll be okay."

Jazelle gave her a meaningful smile. "Sophia and I thought you'd want to know."

A blush stung Tallulah's cheeks and the reaction made her feel silly. Four days had passed since her abbreviated dinner with Jim, and so far she'd not seen or heard from him. But after the way he'd hurried away, she hadn't expected him to contact her.

"Jazelle, you and Sophia are traveling down the wrong track. Jim has no interest in me. None whatsoever. And he's only an acquaintance to me."

Tallulah's effort to appear indifferent was

wasted on the other woman. "You had dinner with him. Or have you forgotten?"

Forgetting Jim would be impossible, she thought. The short time she'd spent with him on the patio was burned into her brain. No matter how hard she tried to push away his memory, she'd found herself remembering each line of his tanned features, the vividness of his blue eyes, the deep timbre of his voice and the way hanks of his tawny hair had fallen waywardly across his forehead. His scent had reminded her of grass and sagebrush damp from a rare rain shower, and she'd instinctively known the fragrance hadn't come from a bottle. Instead, it was his own essence, and she'd been mesmerized by it as much as she'd been charmed by him.

"You and Sophia are obviously suffering from memory lapses. The man couldn't hang around long enough to have dessert with me. Remember?"

Jazelle dismissed Tallulah's reasoning with a wave of her hand. "That's not unusual. Men tend to run from women. Until they finally decide they want to be caught by one."

"I'm hardly trying to catch Jim. I just wanted a bit of his company," Tallulah said, then added with a rueful grimace, "I had a man once, and the misery wasn't worth the effort."

With Madison still attached to her hip, Jazelle sank to her knees on the soft sand and released the hold she had on her daughter. Once the little girl had toddled over to join Abagail, Jazelle folded her legs up under her and turned a wry look on Tallulah.

"I had a real stinker of a man once, too," she said. "So did Sophia. So did a lot of women. But that doesn't mean you put men out of your life forever. Or that all of them are the same."

As Tallulah mulled over Jazelle's words, she thought about her ex-husband and how he'd been a charming rascal from the very beginning. It was her own fault that she'd allowed herself to be blinded by his smooth talk and empty promises.

Glancing at Jazelle, she said, "I don't think all men are like my ex. And I don't intend to put men out of my life forever, either. I'm just…waiting for the right one to come along."

"I'm glad to hear it."

Tallulah laughed. "You and Sophia have to be two of the biggest romantics I've ever known."

"Make that three," Jazelle said. "Your sister-in-law thinks every day is Valentine's Day. But that's a good thing. Right? She's made your brother very happy. And vice versa."

Tallulah nodded. "Tag suffered through some awful times before he came here to Three Rivers. Marrying Emily-Ann is the best thing that ever happened to him."

Before she realized what she was doing, her gaze drifted out to the busy ranch yard. From this vantage point, she could see a section of the red roof of the horse barn, but not the comings and goings of the men. These past few days, she'd caught herself looking in the direction of Jim's workplace and wondering when, or if, she would see him again.

Daydreaming about a man wasn't normal behavior for Tallulah. Since her divorce three years ago, she'd been content to simply work and go about her daily routine with nothing more on her mind than paying the bills and dodging her father's outstretched hand for money, or whatever else he could mooch off her.

But meeting Jim had caused some sort of upheaval in Tallulah. Which made no sense. She'd only been around the man on three occasions. That was hardly enough time to warrant having fantasies about him. But something about the cowboy had put her to thinking about things she'd put on an indefinite hold. Like having a man's love and children of her own.

Tallulah's thoughts were suddenly interrupted when Jazelle stood and brushed sand from the seat of her jeans.

"I'd better get back to work," she announced. Are you sure you don't need me to take Madison? I can clean house and watch her, too."

"No way," Tallulah assured her. "She's having fun."

Jazelle made a palms-up gesture. "I don't want

to take advantage of you. Maureen hired a nanny for her grandchildren. That doesn't include my two kids. Granted, on Connor's off duty days, he watches our son Raine, and with him in second grade now, he's in school all day."

"When Raine is here he's always a good boy. Especially with his little sister. Besides, I've heard Maureen say that she considers Raine and Madison to be her grandchildren, too. And anyway, you're not taking advantage. This is my job. The more kids the merrier."

Jazelle shot her a grateful look. "Maureen didn't hire a nanny. She hired an angel. See you later."

Giving her a little wave, the housekeeper quickly strode across the yard and then disappeared around the corner of the house. Once she was out of sight, Tallulah glanced over at the patio where she and Jim had eaten together.

Jazelle wanted Tallulah to go after the man she wanted, not wait around until he grew tired of running. And maybe in a way her friend was giving her the right advice, she pondered. There couldn't be any harm in seeing Jim again and finding out for herself what kind of man was beneath that rugged exterior. After all, what could it hurt to spend a bit more time with him?

Jim felt a sense of relief when he managed to get a ham and cheese sandwich put together, but as soon as he sat down at the kitchen table to eat, he realized the thing needed to be sliced into smaller pieces in order for him to hold it with one hand.

Muttering a curse word under his breath, he went over to the cabinet and was digging through a drawer for a butcher knife when he heard the doorbell ring.

The sound was such a rarity that it stunned him, and for a moment he stood there frowning, wondering who the heck might be stopping by at this hour of the night.

Tossing the butcher knife onto the counter, he left the kitchen and was halfway across the living room when the bell rang again.

"Hold your horses! I'm here!" he yelled.

After flipping on the porch light, he yanked the door open, then fought like hell not to gasp.

"Tallulah! What are you doing here?"

His blunt greeting put a wry smile on her face. "Hello to you, too."

Embarrassed heat rushed up his neck and onto his face. "Sorry. You surprised me. Uh…please, come in."

She bent down and picked up an insulated carrier bag before she stepped past him and into the house.

While she stood to one side and waited for him to deal with the door, she said, "I'm the one who should be apologizing, Jim. For not calling to let you know I was coming. But I—I thought you might tell me not to come. And then I wouldn't have been able to see for myself that you were okay."

Jim would've never guessed a half-dead heart could beat so fast, but his was suddenly going at the speed of a jackhammer. Why was she here? Had she forgotten he'd behaved like a jerk the other night?

Clearing his throat, he turned to face her and the relentless pounding of the jackhammer jumped to an even faster speed. She looked so soft and feminine with her dark hair coiled into a messy bun and a red-and-white sundress skimming the outline of her curves. A jean jacket was tossed around her shoulders, and Jim hoped the garment remained in place. Considering the swimming sensation in his head, he didn't think he could hold up to the sight of her bare shoulders.

"Why wouldn't I be okay?"

A slight frown pulled her brows together. "Your hand, of course."

"Oh, that." He glanced down at the thick pad of white gauze taped tightly to the palm and fingers of his right hand. "Uh…I guess that's why you figured I'd be home."

Her expression turned to one of amusement. "Well, after getting a bunch of stitches in your hand, I didn't think you'd be out roaming the town tonight."

Jim realized he sounded inane, but seeing her had jolted his senses and so far they'd not yet settled back in place.

"You heard about that?"

"Yes. That your hand had been cut badly."

Actually, seeing her standing on his porch had made him forget all about his hand. But he wasn't about to admit that she had such a strong effect on him. She'd think he was crazy and she'd probably be right, he thought ruefully.

"The numbing shots dulled the pain. The medication is wearing off now, but my hand only has a slight ache. I'll be fine with no permanent damage. You shouldn't have bothered."

"It's really no bother. And it gave me a chance to see where you live." Smiling now, she stepped toward him. "I'm jealous, you know. The view is gorgeous from your front porch. At least, what I could see of it through the dark."

The abrupt change of subject allowed Jim enough pause to gather his scattered senses. "Thanks. I like it."

A soft laugh parted her lips. "My bedroom window looks over a bunch of cottonwood branches and a patch of grass in the yard. But I get to see plenty of birds, so that's nice."

He wasn't being much of a host, Jim realized.

But he'd never had a woman simply show up on his doorstep. An attractive, single woman, at that. How was a man supposed to react?

Clearing his throat, he said, "When you rang the doorbell, I was about to eat a sandwich. Would you care to join me in the kitchen?"

"Thanks. I'd love to join you," she said. "But you can put the sandwich away. I brought dinner. With your injured hand I thought it might be difficult to fix yourself something to eat."

"That was very thoughtful of you, Tallulah." He gestured toward an arched doorway. "The kitchen is right through here."

As the two of them started across the room, Georgette crawled from beneath the couch and made a mad dash across their path.

"Wow! There went an orange flash! Was that your cat?"

He nodded. "That was Georgette. She doesn't trust strangers."

"Obviously," she said with an amused smile.

He gestured for Tallulah to follow him into a hallway, then straight ahead through a single swinging door, and into the kitchen.

As usual the room was cluttered. A few dirty dishes were stacked in the sink, while the makings of his sandwich were scattered across the counter. Near the back door, three pairs of cowboy boots were piled next to a clothes hamper overflowing with dirty garments.

"I apologize for the mess. I guess you can see that I let things pile up before I make myself do any cleaning." Normally, Jim wouldn't have given a second thought to the less than tidy condition of his house. But he didn't want Tallulah to think he was slovenly.

She laughed. "I thought everyone put off cleaning. In fact, I refused to let Jazelle into my bedroom this week because I didn't want her to see how messy I'd been. And I sure didn't want her tidying it up for me. She already has too much to do."

"I'll admit I'm much better at keeping the tack room in the horse barn much neater than my own house," he told her.

A small, white farm table with four matching chairs was pushed against a wall directly across from the cabinets. Jim used his good hand to pull out one of the chairs and gestured for her to take a seat.

"Make yourself comfortable. I'll get plates and something to drink."

Ignoring the chair, she frowned at him and placed the insulated carrier on the table. "Are you kidding? You sit and I'll take care of whatever we need. I came over here to see if there was anything

I could do to help you. Not to have you wait on me like I'm a guest, or something."

If she wasn't his guest, then what was she? He decided it was probably best not to try to answer that question, or to argue with her.

"If that's the way you feel, then there's plates and glasses in the cabinet behind you and silverware in the drawer next to the sink." He aimed a forefinger at the row of cabinets directly behind her.

"Great. I'll find everything."

"There are cans of soda or tea in the fridge. Or if you prefer, the coffee maker is right over your left shoulder, and you'll find the coffee and filters in the cabinet above it."

"I vote for coffee," she said with a grin. "Is that okay with you?"

"Whatever you choose is fine with me."

Seemingly pleased with his answer, she moved over to the cabinets and went to work putting the brew together and gathering dishes and silverware.

While she was busy, Jim pushed the uneaten sandwich aside, then reached for the carrier. Unfortunately, the throbbing pain in his hand made it difficult to open the bag.

He was cursing beneath his breath and attempting to hold the tote steady while unzipping the top when Tallulah called to him.

"Jim! Wait! Let me do that."

He glanced around to see her striding rapidly toward him. From the anxious frown on her face, a person would've thought he'd been about to break an arm or leg.

"I can manage," he stubbornly insisted.

"Is that why sweat has popped out on your forehead?" Her expression was one of wry disbelief as she moved the bag away from him and opened the top. "Sit down, Jim. You look as white as a sheet."

He didn't like the idea of this woman seeing him in a rather helpless condition. A fact that made very little sense. There was no earthly reason he should want to come off to her as a macho man.

He sank into one of the wooden chairs. "I'm finding out that it's not easy doing tasks with only one hand," he admitted.

"That's why I came over tonight. To do these tasks for you." She pulled several plastic containers from the bag and placed them in the middle of the table. "So just relax and I'll get the rest of the things."

Somehow her simple service felt very personal. Like a woman taking care of her man. The feeling very nearly made him squirm. He didn't need a woman doing anything for him. Not since...

"Would you like water to drink along with your coffee? I'll get it for you."

Her question interrupted his straying thoughts, and he mentally shook himself before he darted a glance up at her. "No, thanks. The coffee will be plenty."

With her standing only a few inches away from his side, her feminine scent was drifting over him, reminding him of just how long he'd gone without having a woman in his arms.

"It should be finished dripping by now," she said. "I'll go check."

Once she moved away from him, Jim let out a long breath and tried to tell himself that he wished she'd never knocked on his door. He told himself that all he wanted was for her to hurriedly eat dinner and leave. But he knew he was lying to himself.

The fact that she'd even thought about him being alone with an aching useless hand, touched him in a way he couldn't begin to describe. And just having her in the house had already lifted his flat spirits.

"Did you have this house built?" she asked as she carried two mugs of coffee to the table. "The cabinets are so cute. I guess you'd call them retro—I've not seen any knotty pine cabinets since my grandmother in West Texas was still alive. She had varnished pine cabinets in the kitchen and cedar-lined closets in the bedrooms. I would open the closet doors just to sniff the smell."

She set one of the coffee mugs in front of him and although the urge to turn his head and gaze at her pretty face engulfed him, he forced his eyes to remain locked on the tabletop.

After a moment, she moved away to fetch their plates and realizing he hadn't answered her earlier question, he said, "This house was already here when I first went to work on Three Rivers. I think it was built back in the 1950s, so it's seen a lot of years."

"That's why it has so much character," she told him. "New things are just—well, new. It takes time for anything to build character. Houses, people, even pets. Just like your cat. Over time she's learned she doesn't want to tolerate company."

He grunted with amusement. "Even when Georgette was a young kitten, she didn't like company."

She placed plates and silverware on the table, then sank into the chair next to him. "Maybe she's picked up on your attitude," she suggested.

Her remark brought Jim's head around, and the knowing little smile he found on her lips punched him right in the midsection.

"What does that mean?" he asked.

Smiling faintly, she shrugged one shoulder. "Oh, just that I can tell I'm making you uncomfortable. And that you're probably wishing I'd hurry up and get out of here."

For the second time that evening, he felt a hot

blush creep up his neck. "That isn't what I'm wishing."

A soft laugh escaped her and Jim was so drawn to the sound, he very nearly laughed along with her.

"Then you're wishing I'd never come in the first place." The smile on her face deepened. "Right?"

"Not exactly. And if you want me to be frank, I've actually been wondering why you took time out of your evening to bring dinner to me. Believe me, Tallulah, I've had cuts and bruises and even cracked bones over the years. That kind of thing goes with horse training. So I...wasn't expecting someone like you to show me a little concern."

A bewildered frown puckered her forehead as she lifted the lids off the plastic containers of food and pushed them in his direction. "Someone like me? What does that mean?"

The blush that was already burning his face grew even hotter. "Well, I've hardly been overly friendly. And with you being so pretty and all, I figure you have better choices of men to spend your time with."

This time her laugh was anything but soft. It was ripe and real and made him feel like an even bigger fool.

"Oh, Jim. Well, thank you for the compliment, but you have the wrong idea about me. I'm not swimming in male attention. How could I? I've only been on the ranch for a short while, and the only men I've met are the Hollisters and you."

He picked up his coffee and took a sip in hopes that it would ease the tightness in his throat. "Sounds like you need to get out more."

She shook her head. "I stay fairly busy with the children. And anyway, I'm not on the hunt for a man. I'd rather let fate take care of such things."

Nine years ago his life had been upended when fate had unexpectedly stepped in. He hated to think anyone's life was a tightrope and fate could topple it at any given moment.

"Fate can be brutal," he said flatly as he ladled a large helping of beef stroganoff onto his plate. "You need to remember that."

"Looks like it's something you're not willing to forget."

He paused to stare at her. "You think you can imagine how it feels to be a widower?"

One of her brows lifted ever so slightly, but other than that tiny change in her expression, she appeared undeterred by his blunt question. "You think being a divorcee is easy? You think you can imagine how the demise of my marriage makes me feel?"

"No. But your ex is still alive out there somewhere. If you were so minded to, you could find him and try again. I don't have that option."

She shot him a horrified look, and then she

laughed in a macabre sort of way. "Try again with Shane? I'd rather jump off a forty-foot cliff and land in a prickly pear patch. No, Jim. In my case, there's no going back. The past is the past, and that's where I intend to keep it."

While she helped herself to the food, he wondered if that was her way of saying he should do the same? He should put Lyndsey and baby Cody in the past and keep them there? Well, he could tell her that he'd tried pushing away the memories and looking forward. But that was hard to do when all he could see in his future was a gray fog.

He swiped a hand over his face, then took a long swig of coffee. "Sorry. I had no business saying any of that to you."

"Don't apologize. I had no business saying what I did to you, either. But I'm not sorry I did. I'd like to think we can say whatever we want to each other. That's the way it is with friends, isn't it? You can say what's on your mind and not worry about offending him…or her."

She wanted to be his friend? Oh Lord, how could that possibly work when just looking at her made him go all hot and bothered? She was a man's fantasies come true. She wasn't friend material.

Tallulah might believe they could speak their minds to each other, but it wouldn't work in this case. If she had any idea what he was actually thinking, she'd probably jump up from the table and run out of the house. The same way he'd raced off the patio four nights ago.

Isn't that what you want, Jim? For her to leave so that you can sit here and drown in your misery?

The taunting voice whispering in his ear made his hand ache even worse and turned his already jumbled thoughts into a tangled knot. A part of him did want her to leave and take away all the temptation she was heaping upon him. Yet, he had to admit, an even bigger part of him wanted her to stay. Because as long as she was here by his side, talking to him, it made the pain not quite so unbearable.

Hell. It wasn't his injured hand that was causing him difficulties, he thought. The real problem was his brain and the fact that when Tallulah was near him, he forgot how to use it.

Chapter Five

Jim shook away his wandering thoughts and tried to form a sensible reply to her earlier question.

"I have friends. But there are some things I wouldn't say to them," he told her. "What about you?"

"I have old friends back in Muleshoe. But I only talk with them occasionally. Since I've moved here, I've grown very close to my sister-in-law, Emily-Ann. And to Sophia, Colt's fiancée. If I needed to talk to someone about something private or painful, it would be to one of those two. Or Maureen. She's so wise and brutally honest that I'd trust her opinion on any matter. But I think it's different for women. We're more willing to accept advice because we don't tend to let our egos get in the way."

"Yeah. Men do have big ones." He tried to grin, but the twist of his lips felt more like a smirk.

Thankfully, she was too busy studying his empty plate to notice.

"You've finished your food. Would you like more dessert? There's plenty more cherry pie left."

He didn't know why she was being so kind to him. He wasn't a charming or talkative guy. There were plenty of days he went without speaking more than a handful of words to his coworkers. And his appearance wasn't anything special. So why was she treating him as if he was special?

"Thanks, Tallulah. But to tell you the truth my appetite isn't the greatest. I had to make myself eat everything on my plate because I thought it might make me feel better."

Her brown eyes slipped slowly over him, and Jim was suddenly aware of the stubble he'd not bothered to shave off these past two days. And he didn't need a mirror to show him the lines of fatigue that were undoubtedly etched around his eyes and mouth. He figured he looked like he'd been trampled by a herd of steers.

"Your appetite is gone because you're hurting." Her lips pressed into a thin, disapproving line. "Did the doctor prescribe any painkillers?"

"A few mild ones. I've not taken any, though."

Leaning back in her chair, she folded her arms across her breasts and leveled a pointed look at him. "Why, no. Why would you? It's more important to play tough instead of trying to feel better."

He drew in a deep breath, then blew it out. "Did you take lessons in sarcasm, or something?"

"Sorry. I'd say the 'or something' made me this way. Like dealing with my father."

From the remark Blake had made about Taggart and Tallulah's father, he figured the man was a problem. Now that she'd mentioned him, all sorts of questions raced through Jim's mind. But he kept them to himself. She might not appreciate him prying into her private life. Besides, he had the uneasy feeling that the more he learned about her private life, the more he'd be drawn to her. And getting closer to Tallulah O'Brien wouldn't be a good thing. Not when he was incapable of having a meaningful relationship with any woman.

She suddenly stood, and Jim glanced up just in time to watch her push her chair beneath the table.

"Where's the painkiller?" she asked. "I'll get it for you, and then you should get on the couch and rest."

He'd been expecting her to say she needed to get back to the ranch. The fact that she hadn't caused his brows to lift with surprise.

She laughed at the look of disbelief on his face. "See, I'm not only sarcastic, but I can be bossy, too. When necessary. I think the bossiness comes from giving children their dos and don'ts."

"Great. I've been put in the children's category," he mumbled good-naturedly, then gestured toward a long cabinet door located by a side-by-side refrigerator-freezer. "I put the bottle on the top shelf."

She found the prescription bottle and carried it and a glass of water over to him.

After he'd swallowed the medication, she said, "I really should go and let you get some rest."

Just hearing her mention leaving filled him with disappointment and before he gave himself time enough to think, he said, "It's still early. Why don't we take our coffee out to the living room?"

She smiled at him. "Okay. I'd like that."

After she refilled their cups and the two of them walked out to the living room, where the only light in the room was the glow of a half-moon shining through the picture window. It made for a romantic scene, but Jim didn't want to give her any ideas. He already had too many of his own. Just watching the sway of her dress against her hips as she walked was enough to put all sort of erotic thoughts in his head.

At one end of the couch, Jim switched on a table lamp and waited for her to take a seat before he eased down on the cushion next to her.

"Oh my, what a sight." She spoke softly as her gaze took in the view beyond the window. "Looks like the moon is suspended right over the tips of the mountains. Makes me think we could touch it if we climbed high enough."

Jim had thought the glow of the table lamp would mask the beautiful scene, but the bulb wasn't bright enough to cast a shade over Mother Nature.

"Distance is deceiving out here in the desert," he told her. "Even those mountains are much farther away than you think."

"That's the way it is out on the West Texas plains. The lights of town appear to be close, until you start driving. And then it feels like you've traveled forever before you actually reach them."

She placed the coffee mug on the low table in front of the couch, then pulled off the denim jacket she'd worn over her dress. As she folded the garment and placed it next to the mug, Jim's gaze was drawn to her bare shoulders, the fragile collarbones, and the way the fabric of her dress formed a V between her breasts.

Her tanned skin looked incredibly soft and smooth, and he figured touching it would be like skimming his fingers over a piece of satin. The urge to find out for himself was so strong that he tightened his fingers around the coffee mug and turned his gaze into the far shadows of the room.

"I remember you saying you lived near Prescott." she said. "Does that area look anything like it does here?"

The sound of her voice jarred Jim's rambling thoughts, and it took a moment for his brain to register her questions. "Uh…Prescott? You haven't driven up that way since you moved here?"

"No. I've not really had time for sightseeing. The past few weeks have sort of been a whirlwind. Not that I'm complaining. It's been a nice whirlwind."

If she'd not had a flat tire and he'd been somewhere other than driving the road back to the ranch, the chances of ever meeting her would've been slim. Was that the sort of fate she'd been talking about a few minutes ago? he wondered.

Resisting the urge to clear his throat, he said, "Most folks think Prescott is very pretty. The city lies just south of the Granite Dells or just the Dells as the locals call it."

"You mean valleys? Like hill 'n' dales?"

"No. Not that sort of dale." He spelled out the word for her. "It's an area where huge outcroppings of granite boulders dot the mountains. Other than the lakes and the Dells, the landscape isn't all that different from Yavapai County."

"Sounds interesting. I'll have to make a point to drive up there whenever I get time off. Do you have friends or family there?"

"A few friends who work at the track. My father, Gray, works on a ranch not far from the city. He's a horse wrangler, too."

"So you learned the trade from him?"

He nodded. "Some of my first memories are of

Dad setting me on a horse. I thank God every day for Dad teaching me the trade. The job will never make me rich, but it's rewarding."

"I feel the same way about being a nanny."

The sweet, supportive smile on her face caused Jim to step back in time to when he'd been a young boy and his mother had continually badgered him over his love of horses. She'd never wanted Jim to follow the same path as his father.

You'll never have the drive or fortitude to be anything more than a horse wrangler like your father. Why don't you want to grow up and be somebody? Get a job that will make you wealthy?

He shoved the cutting memories aside and glanced over at Tallulah. She was not like any woman he'd ever known before. Not that he'd known that many. But she had a calm and steady countenance that was as soothing as a warm blanket on a cold night.

"I have a sister, Jacklyn," he told her. "She lives in Prescott and manages a boutique in the downtown area."

Her face brightened with interest. "Oh, you have a sister. Do you two have a close relationship?"

He took a sip of coffee, then returned the mug to the coffee table. "With work keeping us tied up and living some fifty miles apart, we don't often have a chance to see each other. But as siblings go, we're buddies. She's thirty-two. In case you're curious, that's seven years younger than me. Which is quite a bit older than you, I expect."

The corners of her lips tilted upward as though she found his deduction about age amusing. "Not really," she said. "I'm thirty. So see, we're in the same decade."

Jim chuckled. "Sure. You're at one end of the decade and I'm at the other."

"Age is only a number. Our mother often repeated that bit of wisdom. Only, she didn't get the chance to grow old." A shadow crossed her face, but a smile quickly pushed the sad expression aside. "You mentioned your father lived near Prescott. But you haven't said anything about your mother. Is she living?"

Over the years, Jim had tried to purge himself of the bitterness he held toward his mother. He understood that nothing good ever came from harbored resentment. Yet there were times, like tonight, when the old feelings crept up on him.

"Mom is alive and well. But she's no longer married to my father. About the time I entered high school and Jacklyn was a second grader, she divorced Dad and left the area with another man. Later on, she split from him and eventually married someone else."

A thoughtful frown pulled her brows together. "Did she stay involved with you and your sister?"

Jim couldn't hold back a mocking snort. "Once

she left we rarely heard from her and didn't see her at all. But to tell you the truth, it didn't matter to me or Jacklyn. She clearly wanted out of our lives, and no amount of phone calls or letters could make up for deserting us."

A mixture of disbelief and compassion paraded across Tallulah's lovely features. "She turned her back on her own children? Jim, that's…well, it's just terrible."

He shrugged in hopes of appearing indifferent. Yet deep down, it still cut him to the core to recall how his mother had tossed aside her husband and children. Until then, he'd not really known that a parent could just walk away without a backward glance. Her leaving had jarred him and slanted his views about everything.

He let out a heavy breath. "Dad never said much either way about her leaving. He's not the sort of man to keep belaboring a mistake or wrongdoing. But Jacklyn and I were just innocent kids. We didn't understand why we could never do anything to please her or make her proud of us. For a long time we thought there was something wrong with us. As I grew older, I realized Jacklyn and I didn't have a problem. Anita, our mother, is the one who had issues. It took me a while to convince my sister of that, but now that Jacklyn is grown, she understands as well as I do."

"So are you and your sister estranged from Anita now?"

"All of us talk to her on occasion. But to be honest, when I do speak with her it's like I'm trying to make conversation with a stranger." He shook his head. "Actually, speaking with a stranger would probably be easier. All those bad memories wouldn't be standing like a thick wall between us."

She shifted around on the cushion so that she was directly facing him. Jim tried not to notice the movement brought her knee only a scant inch or two away from his. He was also doing his damnedest to ignore the soft, womanly scent emanating from all that bare skin.

"It's the same way with my and Tag's father." She let out a rueful sigh. "I'm usually embarrassed to bring up my father to anyone. But I think you understand what it's like to have a less than stellar parent."

He grunted. "Believe me, Tallulah. I get it."

Regret washed over her features. "I know you do. But it's hard for me to talk about Buck O'Brien. You see, he was and always will be a deadbeat. And mean to the core to go with it. He was horrible to our mother, and all she ever did was work her fingers to the bone to make a home for me and Tag. We feel sure he was the reason for her untimely death of a heart attack. But she was one of those women who was blinded by love. She always forgave him anything."

Blinded by love. Jim could safely say he'd never been that besotted over anyone. Even his feelings for his late wife had been the easy and comfortable kind of love without all the passionate highs and lows.

"I take it she stuck by him," Jim said.

Sighing, she thrust a strand of hair away from her temple. "To the bitter end. Then after she died… well, Buck's source of income was gone, so Tag and I both hoped he'd be forced to find a decent job and stick with it. Unfortunately, he's the sort of man who doesn't want to take orders or break a sweat."

"Has he ever held a job for any length of time?"

"He's a carpenter and a good one when he puts an effort into it. There were times he made decent money working with construction companies around the Hereford-Canyon area. But he's never kept any job for long. Back when Mom was alive, it was easier for him to let her pay the bills while he palled around with his beer-drinking buddies." The grim crease on her forehead deepened. "After Mom died, Buck began scrounging off Tag. Then when Tag finally reached his limit and cut him off, he started coming to me with his hand out—too many times to count. I even had to bail him out of jail once for public intoxication."

"Had to? You should've left him there," Jim said flatly, while trying to imagine this gentle woman dealing with such a loser.

"You're right. But I was embarrassed for people

to learn he was sitting in the Bailey County jail. I wanted to get him out and away from there as quickly as I could."

More interested than he had a right to be, he asked, "What is your father doing now?"

"I don't know. Neither does Tag. We're both holding our breaths that he doesn't show up here. We imagine the only thing stopping him is scraping up the funds to travel here to Arizona."

"You think once he got here, he'd cause trouble?"

Her laugh was caustic. "No. I *know* he'd cause trouble." She shook her head. "I can handle the problem, but I'd hate for the Hollisters to have to deal with him."

The worry of Buck possibly showing up at Three Rivers had to be a constant strain on her, Jim thought. And she didn't deserve to be burdened with that much stress in her life.

"I wouldn't worry about the Hollisters. They're adept at taking care of any kind of situation. And they've been through plenty."

Her sigh was wistful. "That's true. And seeing how deliriously happy Maureen and Gil are together, gives me hope that…"

As her words trailed off, she looked away from him and swallowed hard. And it suddenly struck Jim that she was close to tears. The idea bothered him in ways he didn't want to acknowledge.

When she didn't bother to finish what she'd

been about to say, Jim gently prodded her. "Hope for what?"

Her gaze remained locked on the distant view of the mountains. "Mostly I hope that my broken marriage to Shane hasn't ruined my chance to find happiness. I don't have to tell you, Jim. You already know that being alone isn't easy. And now... well, thinking about trying again is scary." She looked at him. "Isn't that how you feel?"

At this very moment, if someone asked Jim if he was sitting or standing, he couldn't have answered. There was a strange tussle going on inside him, and the urge to move closer to her was rapidly winning the fight with keeping his distance.

"Uh...I don't think about trying again," he said huskily.

She looked straight at him, and Jim's gaze was instantly drawn to the perfect O of her lips.

"Oh. I'm sorry," she murmured.

"Why are you sorry? Because I've given up on romance or because you think you've upset me?"

Even though the lamplight was dim, he could see her face turn a rosy pink. And then with a shake of her head, she scooted closer and placed her hand on his knee. The unexpected touch very nearly caused him to flinch.

"For both," she said softly. "I...uh...I've been thinking a lot about the other night when we had dinner on the patio. And I've decided you left abruptly because I…gave you the wrong impression. Like I was on the prowl for a man. Or I was sizing you up as a boyfriend. I can assure you, Jim, neither of those things are true. I like you, and I'd like to know you better—as a friend. And that's the only reason I'm here tonight."

The touch of her hand was burning a hole right through his jeans. The sensation was fuzzing his brain and making it impossible for him to think with any clarity.

He tried to clear his throat, but even that reflex seemed paralyzed. "I've thought a lot about that night, too, Tallulah," he said hoarsely. "And I do regret one thing."

Her eyes wide with surprise, she made a slow study of his face. "Running away?"

"Okay. Maybe I regret two things," he answered gently. "Running away. And not doing this."

Her smile was like sunshine, and for the first time in years he felt the cold spots inside him begin to warm.

"You mean staying long enough to drink coffee and talk with me?"

"More than that."

As if he'd lost control of his body, his uninjured hand reached out and curved around the warm flesh of her shoulder at the same time his face drew nearer and nearer to hers. Until suddenly all he could see was the fascinating shape of her lips.

"Jim."

His name floated out on a soft whisper, and the sound was so erotic it caused him to groan.

"I should've kissed you the other night, Tallulah. I wanted to taste your lips. But I was afraid to."

"Why were you afraid? Did you think I wouldn't kiss you back?"

"No. I was afraid I'd like it…far too much."

Her hands came up to cradle the sides of his face, and that was all it took to make everything in the room fade away, except her and the indescribable longing rushing through his body.

"Oh, Jim."

He didn't know whether she made the final move to connect their lips, or if he did. Either way, it hardly mattered. Suddenly he was kissing her, and the honey sweetness of her lips was consuming him with waves of pleasure.

Sensations were racing through Tallulah at full throttle. There were so many, in fact, that she found it impossible to concentrate on just one single pleasure. Instead, she tried to drink them all in at once, until every thought in her head began to spin and blur.

Mindlessly, she slipped her arms around his neck and opened her mouth to deepen the kiss. His hard lips tasted faintly of salt and coffee, but mainly they tasted like man. A man who wanted her. The idea was exhilarating and filled her with the need to have his hard body pressed to hers. To have his lips crushing down on hers until breathing was impossible. Until she didn't care if she ever took another breath.

In an effort to get closer, she shifted her body until her breasts were smashed against his chest and one of her legs had slipped between his knees. Somewhere above the roaring in her ears she heard him groan, and then his tongue was prodding against her teeth, urging her to open the intimate cavity to him.

As soon as his tongue slipped inside, a shaft of red-hot desire shot straight to her inner core, and as it continued to burn, she realized she didn't just want to kiss him. She wanted to make love to him completely and totally.

And he must've been having those same thoughts, because suddenly the circle of his arms was tightening around her. At the same time, the thrust of his tongue was growing bolder and hungrier as it explored the ribbed roof of her mouth and traced the sharp edges of her teeth.

Lack of oxygen was burning her lungs, but she ignored the pain. If she kissed him for hours without stopping, it wouldn't be enough. If she made love to him over and over, it would only whet her appetite for more.

The wild, sensual thoughts were darting through

her head when suddenly he lifted his mouth from hers and turned his face aside.

"What in hell are we doing?" he asked, his voice gruff with desire.

She sucked in several ragged breaths before she was composed enough to speak. "I believe it's called kissing."

"That was more than kissing!"

His words made her flaming cheeks even hotter. "I was thinking the same thing. And it was… incredible. Didn't you think so?"

"Incredible, yes. Sensible, no." He looked incredulous.

Every cell in Tallulah's body was yelling at her to plaster another heated kiss on his lips, to make him forget all about practicality. But she wasn't about to follow through on the urge. Not when he already looked as though he was ready to bolt.

She said, "Chemistry isn't supposed to be sensible. That's the magic of it."

His groan was full of misgivings as he eased away from her and rose from the couch. Tallulah couldn't have felt more rejected as she watched him walk over to the picture window and stand with his back to her.

"I guess you're telling me that you regret kissing me."

His gaze remained on the window. "No. I don't regret it. But it damned sure worries me."

Tallulah pushed herself off the couch and walked over to him. "Why? Is there something about me that you don't like? Be honest."

He turned toward her and as his good hand wrapped over the top of her shoulder, it was all she could do to stop herself from stepping closer and slipping her arms around him.

"That's a silly question."

"Is it?"

His lips twisted to a wry slant. "A couple of minutes ago, I thought I'd made my feelings pretty obvious. I like everything about you. In fact, I'm damned attracted to you."

His admission should've given her hope. Instead, the look on his face left her wary. "If that's the case, why do you look miserable?"

His hand lifted from her shoulder to make a weary swipe over his face. "I've been a bachelor for a long time. I've turned off the idea of being with a woman."

"It didn't feel like you were turned off when you were kissing me."

A pained look crossed his face, and Tallulah understood the reaction had nothing to do with his injured hand.

"That's because for a few minutes I forgot myself," he muttered.

"I forgot myself, too. I tend to do that when I'm around you."

His blue gaze latched on to hers. "You'd be wasting your time on me, Tallulah."

The poignant tone to his voice brought stinging tears to the back of her eyes. And before she realized what she was doing, her palms were cradling his jaws.

"Maybe I would be," she said softly.

His brows pulled together. "Then what are you doing here with me?"

"I like you, Jim. A lot. I like being with you. I don't exactly know where that might take us. Not any more than you do. Because...well, for the past few years I've turned a blind eye to men. But something made me look at you."

His eyes searched hers, as if they could give him the answers he needed. Tallulah could only hope he couldn't see how madly attracted she was to him. If he guessed how much she wanted to make love to him, he'd no doubt run faster and farther than he had the night of their dinner on the patio.

"Tallulah, I—"

"You don't have to say it, Jim." She interrupted before he could go on. "I understand you haven't had any desire to have a woman in your life. But this chemistry between us—or whatever you want to call it—is not something we ought to ignore or just throwaway. We might be throwing something wonderful away."

His gaze fell to her lips and everything inside Tallulah quivered with longing.

"I like you, too. And I'd be lying if I said I didn't want to spend more time with you. Because, wise or not, I do want to get to know you better."

She curbed the urge to jump up and down with joy. Instead, she leaned in and placed a soft, lingering kiss upon his lips.

By the time she eased her head back, his brows were arched into two question marks.

"That's to seal the deal," she explained.

His expression softened. "You're a hard woman to figure, Tallulah."

She flashed him a pointed smile. "Then that makes us equal. Because I'm finding it impossible to figure you."

Easing away from him, she headed toward the doorway leading to the kitchen.

"Where are you going?"

"To deal with your dirty kitchen," she told him. "And don't start arguing. Once your hand has healed you can wash the dishes."

She was halfway across the room, when a flash of orange fur darted across the floor and came to a skidding halt at her heels.

"Georgette! Have you decided you want to say hello?" Tallulah squatted on her heels and held her palm out to the inquisitive cat.

"Watch out," Jim warned. "She's temperamental. She might claw you. I have the scars on my hands to prove it."

Undeterred by the warning, she gently rubbed Georgette between the ears. The cat purred and rubbed her cheek against Tallulah's hand. "She isn't going to claw me. She's learned much quicker than you that I'm a friend."

Smiling faintly, he walked over to her and the cat. "Felines have nine lives. They can afford to take more chances than us humans."

Chuckling, she rose to her full height and curled her arm around his. "Come on," she told him. "While I clean, you can sit and tell me where everything goes."

Jim never grew tired of the busy sights and sounds of the horse barn. From long before daylight until darkness shrouded the huge building and connecting corrals, there were cowboys calling to each other, horses neighing and stomping for their meals, and the never-ending stream of music from a transistor radio. Even the mingled odors of leather, wood shavings, horse hair and manure were comforting scents he associated with the place he considered more of a home than the actual house he lived in.

Presently, the stalled horses had already eaten their breakfasts and were outside getting their exercise on portable walkers. Meanwhile barn workers were busy mucking out stalls and laying down clean shavings. As for Jim, he'd already saddled three horses for Luke and Colt to ride in the training arena, along with making sure there were enough boiled oats in the feed room to take care of the horses that received noonday rations.

"Jim, what in hell are you doing here today?"

At the sound of Holt's voice, Jim turned from the fourth horse he'd begun saddling a few minutes ago, to see his scowling boss bearing down on him. At seven thirty, Jim had already been at work for two hours. Normally, Holt arrived at the horse barn around five or shortly after, but since Isabelle had gotten pregnant again, he'd been helping his wife with chores at Blue Stallion before he left for Three Rivers.

"I do work here."

"Not when you're hurt!" He gestured to Jim's heavily bandaged hand. "Colt told me what the doctor said. He doesn't want you doing any kind of movement that might rip those stitches open. How did you get the saddle on the horse's back, anyway?"

"I lifted it up there. Just like I do two dozen times or more a day. And quit fussing over me like a mother hen. I'm being careful. Nothing is ripped open."

Holt rolled his gaze up to the rafters. "Since

you're already here, I'm not going to bother sending you home."

"Good. I wouldn't go anyway," Jim told him. "Colt needs more help than usual now that he's stove-up with a cracked collarbone."

Holt pinched the bridge of his nose and let out a heavy breath. "Colt shouldn't be riding at all. But I can't seem to make him follow doctor's orders, either. You two are pains in the butt, you know it?"

Jim grinned. "How many times have I seen you ride with a cast on your arm, or ankle, or your ribs taped tight? You're the last person who ought to be talking about following doctor's orders."

Holt's smile was full of guilt. "Well, it's different with me."

"Sure. It's okay for you to behave like a risky fool, but not your employees."

Holt grunted with amusement, then glanced toward his right where a barn worker was pushing a wheelbarrow piled high with manure and dirty shavings.

"How long have the horses been out on walkers?"

Jim glanced at his watch. "About twenty minutes."

"We may have to bring them in early. I know it's unlikely, but as I was driving over here, I noticed some thunderheads gathering to the west. They might hang over the mountains, but you never know," he said. "Is Colt already in the training arena?"

"He was. But right now he's gone to the mares' paddock. He said something about a feeling he was having about Sugar."

Holt frowned. "Sugar's foal isn't due for a while. He must be picking up on something about the mare that I missed. I'll talk with him after I make a few phone calls."

Holt took off in the direction of his office, but after a few strides, stopped and looked over his shoulder at Jim.

"By the way, a little bird told me you had dinner with Tallulah the other night. How did that go?"

Their meal together on the patio had been five days ago. Why was Holt just now bringing that up? Because Holt had somehow found out that Tallulah had visited Jim at his house last night?

Turning toward the horse, Jim reached for the leather girth strap and used his good hand to pull it upward. "I'll just bet your little birdie was none other than Colt."

Holt chuckled. "My source of information doesn't matter. What I want to know is whether you enjoyed your time with her."

If Holt had any idea of how much he enjoyed being with Tallulah, the man would be shocked. Even so, he wouldn't be nearly as much as Jim was shocked at himself. That wild kiss they'd shared on the couch last night was still rattling his peace of mind. He'd not imagined he could want a woman quite that much. He'd believed his body and his mind had totally shut down to the idea of sex. Hell, he couldn't have been more wrong, or more stupid.

"Tallulah is a nice lady. And very pretty to go with it. Why wouldn't I enjoy being with her?"

Holt walked back over to Jim's side. "I'm asking, Jim, because I'm straining to remember the last time you've had a date. It's been so damned long I've forgotten."

Actually, Jim had forgotten himself. That's how uneventful his attempts at dating had been. "You know me, Holt. Dating never has been on my agenda."

"When Colt told me about you and Tallulah, I was hoping all of that had changed," Holt said frankly.

Rather than face Holt, Jim continued to tighten the girth. "I know you'd like for me to become a family man. But that part of my life is over. Maybe I can enjoy spending some time Tallulah. That's about all I can hope for."

"Damn it, Jim. Nothing is over. Your life could be beginning again. If you'd just let it."

Turning, Jim leveled a pointed look at Holt. "There's nothing wrong with my life as it is. I love my job. And all you Hollisters treat me like family. I don't need more."

"Don't give me that baloney. Your bed is empty.

Your house is empty. You need a woman and children of your own."

Not long after Jim had come to work at Three Rivers, he'd talked to Holt, and only Holt, about Lyndsey and how she'd lost her life in a freak horse accident. But Jim hadn't found the fortitude to go one step further and reveal the facts of losing his son after six short days of life. And to this day, Holt, or anyone else on the ranch, didn't know about baby Cody. The loss was his own private hell. One that he couldn't share.

"You know how I feel, Holt," he said tightly. "After losing Lindsay…well, I don't want to take a chance on losing again."

The deep grimace on Holt's face made it clear he was disappointed by Jim's attitude. "I admit I've never gone through what you have, Jim. I can only imagine the pain. But you're turning your back on a chance for happiness. And that's damned wrong. For a lot of reasons."

Jim opened his mouth to argue, but Tallulah's image shoved its way into his thoughts and suddenly he was seeing her sparkling smile, hearing her soft voice.

"You're right, Holt. Heck, I can admit that. But—" Pausing, he let out a groan of resignation. "Okay, I might as well tell you—Tallulah came over to see me last night."

Holt's stare was blank until he registered Jim's

words, and then a grin spread across his face. "I'm going to assume you didn't invite her. I can't imagine you doing anything that *normal*."

"She came over to bring dinner and check on my hand. To see if I needed help—or anything."

"I see. To give you a little nursing. Well, I hope you told her you were going to need lots of it—nursing, that is," he added slyly.

Jim frowned. "Look, Holt. You're an expert on women. I'm not. So everything I said to her probably didn't make much sense. But we...uh...agreed it would be nice for us to be friends."

"That's all? Friends?"

"We've only just met," Jim said defensively. "Anyway, she's nine years younger than me. And way too pretty and nice for a saddle tramp like me."

Holt laughed. "Some women like saddle tramps. Just ask Isabelle. She's about to give me my third child. That ought to tell you something."

It did tell Jim something. That if he wasn't very careful, his feelings would get all tangled up with Tallulah. And he couldn't allow that to happen. He couldn't allow himself to dream and hope and love again. The risk to his heart was too much of a gamble.

Chapter Six

"Nanny Tally, I want to wear my pink dress for dinner. The one with the bows. Like Abby's."

Tallulah finished laying out a fresh set of underwear on Evelyn's half bed before she turned to the little girl. After taking a shower only a minute ago, the child was bundled in a white terry-cloth robe and her blond hair hung in wet ringlets down her back.

Presently, Katherine was looking after the twins, and Billy was already dressed and occupied with his toys in the playroom. Evelyn was the last to get ready before the whole family went downstairs for the evening meal.

"Are you talking about the dress with bows up here?" Tallulah tapped the top of her own shoulder.

Evelyn nodded eagerly. "That's the one. Abby

is going to wear hers tonight, too. And I want to look as pretty as she does."

Because Abagail was slightly older, Evelyn wanted to emulate her cousin as much as possible. Tallulah had never had a big sister or a female cousin to look up to. Now that she was caring for the Hollister children, she was seeing for herself just how much she and Taggart had missed by growing up with very few relatives.

"You know something, Evie?" Tallulah walked over and touched the tip of her finger to Evelyn's little freckled nose.

"No. What?"

"No matter what dress you wear, you're just as pretty as Abagail."

A wide smile spread across the child's face. "Is that really true, Nanny Tally?"

"It's very true," Tallulah answered. "But you need to understand there's something else that's just as important as being pretty."

Evelyn's head tilted from side to side as she contemplated Tallulah's remark. "Oh, I know what that is. Being nice. That's important."

Tallulah gave the girl a smile of approval. "Being nice is definitely important. So is being smart. And I think you're a very smart girl."

Evelyn trotted over to the full-length mirror attached to a closet door, and as Tallulah watched the girl peer closely at her image, the question of having her own children pushed its way into her thoughts. Since she'd come to work at Three Rivers, the idea of becoming a mother had struck her far more often than when she'd lived in Muleshoe.

She supposed seeing the Hollister families so happy and in love made the whole notion of being a wife and mother seem idyllic. But her one attempt at having a family life had failed miserably. She and Shane had never had a conventional marriage. Actually, they'd never had a real marriage, she thought ruefully. In the beginning she'd believed it to be real and she'd invested her whole heart into making a home and family with her new husband. Yet she'd quickly learned he wasn't interested in domestic life or being faithful to her.

"Nanny Tally, do I look smart?"

The child's question pulled Tallulah from her dismal thoughts. She walked over to Evelyn and gently patted the top of her head. "Smart enough to be anything you want to be when you grow up."

"Wow! That's super!"

"It's super, all right." She placed her hands on the girl's shoulders and turned her toward the bed. "But right now you need to hurry and get dressed. You want to be ready to go downstairs at the same time Abby goes, don't you?"

"Oh, yeah!"

Evelyn began pulling on her clothes, and Tallulah stood to one side to allow the child to do the task.

While she waited, the phone in her shirt pocket vibrated to announce an incoming message. Since Roslyn was running late getting home from her workday at the animal hospital, Tallulah expected the text to be from her. However, when she pulled out the phone and quickly scanned the screen, she found a message from Jazelle.

We need you in the kitchen in twenty minutes.

Frowning faintly, Tallulah tapped out the word *okay*, then slipped the phone back into her shirt pocket.

Why was she needed in the kitchen? Jazelle was so efficient at serving drinks and dinner, she rarely needed help with that particular job. And Jazelle's husband, Connor, who was a deputy sheriff and Joseph Hollister's partner, was off duty this evening and caring for Madison and Raine. So the housekeeper didn't need Tallulah to watch her children.

"I can't do this, Nanny Tally. Will you help me?"

Tallulah stepped over to Evelyn, and as she tied the shoulder straps on the girl's sundress, she told herself it didn't matter why she was needed in the kitchen. Once the children were having dinner with their parents, Tallulah's nanny duties would be over for the evening and she had nothing else planned.

Even though there was something she wanted to do. And that something had been on her mind ever since she'd rolled out of bed this morning. She wanted to see Jim again. The problem was, she wasn't about to drive over to his house un-invited for a second night in a row. He'd get the idea she was chasing him. And that wouldn't work at all. The man was hard to read, but she could see enough to understand he wouldn't appreciate her throwing herself at him. Besides, in Tallulah's opinion, any man that had to be chased wouldn't be worth the effort.

Jim was in the tack room making sure all the saddles and accompanying tack used earlier in the day was put up and accounted for when Holt stepped through the door.

"Hey, Jim, what are you planning to do? Spend the night in the barn?"

Jim glanced from Holt to the watch on his wrist, then walked over to where Holt was standing just inside the open doorway. "It's not that late. I was just making sure all the saddles have been brought in from the training arena."

Holt looked pointedly at Jim's hand where, earlier in the day, blood had seeped through the thick gauze.

"I'm not happy with what I see. You need to get

home and change that dressing on your hand. If you've torn a stitch, I'm going to kick your butt."

"Don't worry, Holt. I'll see to it. The doctor told me what to do about changing the bandage, and I have some prescription salve for the cut."

"Good. See that you do it. In the meantime, Mom has sent word for you to stop by the kitchen. Reeva's packing a box of dinner for you."

Jim shot him a skeptical glance. "Why would Maureen have the cook go to all that trouble? I can make myself something with one good hand. Or I can always stop by the bunkhouse and eat with the guys."

Holt frowned. "Don't argue. Mom said if you don't stop by the house, she'll fire you."

Jim rolled his eyes. He'd worked too long for the Hollisters to know that Maureen wouldn't fire any hand unless they done something incredibly negligent or criminal. "She actually said that?"

Holt's grin was a bit sheepish. "Well, not exactly. But she was firm, so you better do as you're told and not make her angry. All you have to do is knock on the kitchen door, and someone will be there to hand you everything. You won't even have to go inside."

"Okay. I guess I can manage that. But I don't want any of the other ranch hands to hear about this. They'll be accusing me of getting special treatment."

Holt chuckled. "Everyone around here gets special treatment—whenever they deserve it. Now get gone. All the horses are where they should be, and Colt will check everything here in the barn before he leaves. I'll see you tomorrow," he said.

"Yeah, tomorrow," Jim replied.

Holt turned and strode off in the direction of his office. Jim shut the door of the tack room and headed toward the far end of the barn where his truck was parked outside the side exit door.

Having another home-cooked meal like the one he'd had last night, he thought, as a couple of minutes later, he steered his truck past the cattle barn and on toward the big ranch house. But he was a bit concerned what he'd do if he ran into Tallulah.

Throughout the day, she'd continually popped into his thoughts, and he'd found himself reliving the taste of her lips and the way her soft body had felt pressed against his.

He didn't understand why kissing her, touching her had felt so different, so unforgettable. It wasn't like she was the first woman he'd touched in all the years since Lyndsey had died, because he'd had touched and kissed and gone through the motions of having sex with a few women he'd dated. But those encounters had only left him feeling emptier and lonesome. When Tallulah's lips had touched his, he'd felt something spark and ignite. He'd felt something real. And God help him, he wanted to experience the wonder of her kiss again.

Several times today, he'd considered calling or texting Tallulah to thank her again for dinner and cleaning his kitchen. But he'd hesitated, because he'd known just as sure as his middle name was Johnson that the contact would cause him to end up inviting her to come over to his house tonight. And he wasn't sure what she'd think about spending time with him so soon after last night. Would she want to waste her time on a man who'd practically forgotten how to talk with a woman?

Images of Tallulah were still swirling through his head when he parked behind the Hollisters big ranch house. As he walked across the yard, he glanced over at the patio where the two of them had shared dinner. Presently, the covered area was dark and empty, while the play area where the children's gym set and sandpile were located was deserted and quiet.

Everyone was inside, enjoying being together, Jim thought. Blake was probably making a fuss over his pregnant wife, insisting that Katherine put up her feet and rest after working at school all day. From what Holt had said, Blake had tried hard to talk Katherine into quitting her job as secretary to Prudence Crawford, who was superintendent at St. Francis private school in Wickenburg. But

Katherine loved her job and only agreed to cut her work down to three days a week rather than five.

Jim had felt the same way when Lyndsey had been pregnant. He'd wanted to coddle and protect her. And when she'd insisted that she wanted to keep riding her horses, he'd not been able to stop her. She'd continued to race barrels until her fifth month. And then to his relief, she'd decided to take a break from the sport and quit riding until after the baby was born. Still, that hadn't been enough to save her and their son.

Frustrated that the dark thought had suddenly struck him, Jim gave himself a hard mental shake, then knocked on the back door.

After a moment, he heard footsteps approach and then the door creaked open to show Tallulah standing in the open space. She was holding a rather large cardboard box, and the warm smile on her face was exactly the same as he remembered.

"Hi, Jim."

Rattled by the sight of her, he looked at her with comical confusion. "Tallulah. Have you started working in the kitchen?"

She laughed lightly. "Not yet. I think Reeva and Sophia might be a little leery of letting me cook anything. I brought your dinner to the door because everyone is busy."

"Oh, well I hope I didn't interfere with whatever you were doing."

"You haven't interfered with anything. I'm off duty now." She carefully balanced the box on one hip as she stepped onto the porch. "If you'll shut the door for me, I'll carry this out to your truck for you."

"Why?" he asked as he quickly took care of the door. "I can carry it myself. I've saddled horses all day. I can surely carry a box of food."

She shot him another wide smile, and he thought how pretty she looked with her dark hair pulled into a ponytail high on the back of her head and a swipe of pink color on her lips.

"So can I. So just follow me and don't worry," she told him. "I won't think you're weak or helpless if you let me help you."

Seeing she was determined to carry the box, Jim decided not argue. Especially when it gave him a reason to have her company for another minute or two.

"First Maureen wants to feed me. Now you want to carry the meal to my truck. I hope Colt keeps his mouth shut about this. I'll never live it down if the other ranch hands get wind of it."

She laughed as the two of them started walking across the yard toward the gate that led out to the parking area.

"With Colt coming to eat in the kitchen with Sophia every evening, we hear about all kinds of things that go on in the horse barn. But I think that's as far as his talk goes." She darted a smile at him. "I can tell Colt thinks highly of you. He says Holt couldn't do without you and neither could him or Luke. That's quite a compliment."

"Colt is just being a nice guy. What I do with the horses most anyone can do."

"You won't convince me of that. Otherwise, you wouldn't be head wrangler of the biggest ranch in Texas."

Uncomfortable with her praise, Jim couldn't think of a suitable reply, so he remained silent.

As they continued to walk on, she asked, "How did things go with your hand today? I bet Holt was annoyed with you for not staying home."

He glanced at her. "I'm not one to miss work for any reason. But I'll admit today hasn't been easy. Not with trying to do things one-handed."

They reached the truck and Jim opened the back door so that she could place the box on the floorboard. As she leaned past him, the scent of her perfume drifted to his nostrils, and he was struck with the urge to drop his face to the curve of her neck and drink in the warm flowery smell.

"There. That should ride without tipping," she said. "As long as you don't slam on the brakes. Anyway, everything should still be hot by the time you get home. Sophia packed the food in thermal containers like those I took to your house last night. So you won't have to deal with putting anything in the microwave."

She stepped back from the truck, and he shut the door before he turned to her.

"That's nice," he said, then awkwardly shifted his weight from one boot to the other. "Uh…have you eaten yet?"

"No. Roslyn was late getting home from the clinic so that caused me to work a bit longer this evening. I haven't had a chance to dig into the chicken and dumplings. They smell scrumptious, by the way."

Jim wondered if something had caused his tongue to stick to the roof of his mouth. Because try as he might, he couldn't seem to make it work.

After a few seconds passed without a reply from him, she frowned with faint amusement. "Why are you looking at me like that? Is my lipstick smeared or something?"

He wished she hadn't mentioned lipstick. The thought of actually kissing the pink color from her lips had already been rolling around in his mind.

Clearing his throat, he finally managed to make his tongue work. "No. I'm sorry. I didn't mean to stare. I was only wondering if…you'd like to come over to the house and eat dinner with me? I imagine there's enough for two people in that box."

A light flashed in her eyes, and then a happy smile spread over her face. "I'd love to, Jim. If you truly mean it."

Working seven days a week at the ranch didn't

give Jim much time or energy to entertain company. But having Tallulah around was entirely different.

"I'd like it if you'd come," he told her.

She glanced thoughtfully down at her skirt and blouse, then toward the house. "Okay. Give me a moment to get my phone and purse, and I'll follow you in my truck."

He shook his head. "No need for you to bother with your truck. I'll drive you back here whenever you're ready to come home."

Her brows lifted slightly. "Oh, that's too much trouble for you."

"No trouble at all," he assured her.

Smiling, she said, "Okay. I'll go get my things and let Sophia know that I'm going with you."

Minutes later, Tallulah was snuggled comfortably in the leather passenger seat of Jim's truck as he drove them off Three Rivers property and turned at the junction where the ranch road met another county dirt road.

Although the sun had slipped behind the distant mountains a few minutes ago, there was still enough lingering twilight to see the passing terrain of rock spirals, tall saguaros standing with their arms lifted skyward, and random patches of thorny chaparral and prickly pear.

Tallulah never tired of the beautiful view. However, the landscape was hardly the thing on her mind as they traveled toward Jim's house. Her mind was buzzing with questions. Mainly, why he'd invited her to share his dinner. Was he thinking to pay her back for cleaning his kitchen? Or had he found it impossible to forget her kiss?

Don't waste your time wondering about the whys, Tallulah. Just enjoy the fact that Jim wanted your company.

"I haven't asked you how your work went today," he said. "Were the kids rowdy?"

His voice interrupted the mental lecture going off in her head, and glad for the reprieve, she looked in his direction.

"Not today," she answered. "It helps that the four oldest are in preschool. So in the mornings, after I see them onto the special school bus that only transports the very young students, I go back home and tend to Madison. Sometimes Emily-Ann brings Brody over for me to watch him while she runs Conchita's. But only when she knows I'm not extremely busy."

"Brody" he repeated thoughtfully. "That's your little nephew."

Nodding, Tallulah chuckled. "He is quite a firecracker. Let me tell you, his red hair goes along with his personality. He's crazy about Billy. And when you put the two boys together—oh my gosh, it's a circus." She glanced over at his profile, which was illuminated by the lights on the dash panel.

"But aside from dealing with the kids today, I did think of you and wonder if you were taking extra care with your hand."

He grimaced. "I don't think I did anything to damage it more. But it's damned aggravating not to be able to do farrier work. Holt has a blacksmith come in once or twice a month to do whatever is needed. But in between those times, there are always hooves to be trimmed, or shoes that come loose and need to be reset. I'm the guy who take care of those tasks. But now that I can't put that much pressure on my hand, Luke is having to take care of those jobs. And he already has a big load on his shoulders."

Jim was clearly a man who took pride in his work, Tallulah thought. And not for any reason did he want someone else to shoulder his responsibilities. The fact spotlighted many of the differences she'd already noticed between Jim and her ex. Shane had never felt bothered or guilty to have a coworker fill in for him just because he wanted to slough off a day.

"The men understand the situation, Jim. And you'll be back to a hundred percent before long."

"I hope you're right, Tallulah. It's a helpless feeling when you can't carry your own weight."

"Look on the bright side," she told him. "Better that the horse kicked your hand rather than your head."

He glanced at her. "Yeah. Be thankful for my blessings. Right?"

For the first time since she'd met Jim, his smile reached his eyes and seeing his lighter mood caused her spirits to soar.

"Now you're talking," she answered.

Jim's house was an L-shaped structure with cedar siding and dark brown trim around the windows and gables. A covered porch ran the full length of both wings, with the roof being supported by large cedar posts. A carport, wide enough for two vehicles, was attached to the right side of the building, while directly behind it stood a cotton-wood tree and few smaller junipers.

After Jim parked the truck and they departed the vehicle, Tallulah retrieved the box of food from the back floorboard, then followed him to the house.

A row of solar ground lamps lit up a walkway to the porch, where another motion light flashed as they walked across the planked floor. While Jim unlocked the door, Tallulah glanced around her and thought how homey the place looked with a group of yellow lawn furniture facing the front lawn and a blooming rosebush climbing up a fat corner post.

Back in Muleshoe, Tallulah had tried to think of her house as a home, but Shane had only treated it as a stopping off place between his jobs in the oil-fields. Living mostly alone had made the house feel like nothing more than a collection of rooms. On the other hand, now that she resided in the Three Rivers Ranch house, she was surrounded by a huge family. Yet it wasn't actually her family. And the big three-story house wasn't really her home, either.

"Come on in," Jim said, putting on a light. "You might want to watch out for Georgette, though. She can get underfoot at times."

As they made their way into the living room, Tallulah asked, "Do you think Georgette will remember me?"

He paused to switch on a table lamp. "She'll remember. But she'll treat you like a stranger. That is, until you make a fuss over her. She's a diva."

Tallulah chuckled. "I wonder where she got that attitude?"

"I'm clueless. I've told her she comes from a family of barn cats. But I don't think she believes me. I even threaten to take her back to the barn at times. But she doesn't believe that, either."

They walked on to the kitchen, where Jim promptly switched on a fluorescent light above a double sink. As Tallulah glanced around the room, she noticed a small radio atop the refrigerator was playing music at a low volume.

"You forgot to turn off your radio," she told him as she placed the cardboard box on the table.

"While I'm at work I leave it on to give Georgette company."

"Hmm. I'm beginning to see where she gets the idea she's royalty. Jim, you're a softie."

Grinning sheepishly, he walked over and switched off the radio. "Well, I've promised her a boyfriend, too. But so far I don't think any of the male barn cats at the ranch meet her standards."

Tallulah started to laugh when she suddenly spotted his bandaged hand. Now that the two of them were actually in a brightly lit space, she could see the gauze was stained with large splotches of dried blood.

Without a second thought, she hurried over and took hold of his arm.

"Jim, your hand has been bleeding. Let me see!"

Gently cradling his injured hand between her palms, she lifted it for a closer inspection.

"It hasn't bled for a while now."

She shot him a skeptical frown. "Is that supposed to reassure me?"

"I'm not like Georgette," he said with wry amusement. "I don't need to be fussed over."

She lifted her gaze to his face and instantly found herself mesmerized by the shape of his chiseled lips, the faint dent in his chin and the vivid blue of his eyes. A stubble of brown whiskers shadowed his upper lip and jaws and gave his rugged features an even earthier appearance.

"What if I want to fuss over you?"

His gaze fell to her lips and Tallulah felt her heart lurch into a wild gallop.

"I…uh…have the feeling I couldn't stop you," he murmured. "Even if I wanted to."

Was he going to kiss her? Throughout the day she'd not been able to shake the memory of his lips moving over hers, the erotic taste of his mouth and how his hands had spread warmth to each spot they'd touched. The longing to experience all of those sensations a second time refused to leave her. And now that the two of them were alone, with only a scant inch or two separating their bodies, she was struggling to hang on to her composure.

She cleared her throat, but it did little to remove the raspy note from her voice. "Your feeling is correct. And right now, before we eat, I think we should do something about getting this hand cleaned."

"Okay. Everything needed to do that is in the bathroom."

She eased his hand back to his side. "Then lead the way."

They left the kitchen, and Tallulah followed him down a short hallway until they reached a door on the right.

Inside the roomy bathroom, Jim switched on a row of lights above the vanity mirror, then pulled out the things needed to redress his hand. The collection included a large roll of gauze, adhesive tape, small surgical pads, a cleansing antiseptic, scissors and a tube of medication.

"I think that's everything," he said, then laid his hand, palm up, on top of the vanity cabinet. "I'd better warn you that this is kinda ugly. If blood or wounds make you queasy, better let me take care of it."

"Nonsense. I have a strong constitution. It's necessary when you're dealing with kids," she added with an impish grin. "I can handle this."

She picked up the small scissors and carefully begin to snip at the dirty bandage on his hand. All the while, she was keenly aware of his hard masculine body standing a tiny space from hers, the scent of alfalfa and horse drifting from his clothes, and the soft sound of his breathing alternating with the rhythm of her own.

"This might surprise you, but I've actually taken first-aid classes," she said in an effort to distract her thoughts. "Something else that goes along with child care. You have to be ready for all kinds of accidents."

When he remained silent, she glanced up and found a grimace on his face. Puzzled by the expression, she asked, "Am I hurting you?"

"No. I was just thinking about…something. Don't worry about hurting me. Go ahead and do what you have to do."

Apparently, he had no intentions of explaining

what that something was that he'd been thinking about, and Tallulah figured she was better off not knowing. She'd already decided that Jim was a bit of an enigma. In fact, she imagined he was the kind of person who never allowed anyone to know what was actually going on in his head. As for his heart, he probably kept it under lock and key.

"I'll try to be gentle," she said, and turned her focus back to removing the bandage.

Once she finally had the soiled gauze and tape removed from his hand, she found a thin solid pad lying against the actual cut. After carefully peeling it away, she peered closely at the long, wicked looking gash that ran in a crooked angle starting from just below his forefinger all the way to the heel of his palm.

In a hushed tone, she said, "This looks awful."

"You mean awful like infected? Or awful like it's a bad gash?"

"It's certainly a bad gash. But I don't see any infection. And all the stitches look snug and secure." Shaking her head, she looked up at him. "I honestly don't know how you worked today. Obviously, each time you flex your hand it causes the wounded flesh to move."

"I'll be honest. It's been hell. But if you tell anybody I said that, I'll call you a liar."

She rolled her eyes good-naturedly. "Okay,

tough guy. I'll not say anything to put your steel image in danger."

Returning her attention to her job, she reached for the antiseptic and for the next few minutes she gingerly cleaned his whole palm, then smoothed antibiotic ointment directly over the wound.

He didn't speak throughout the process, and Tallulah wondered how he felt about her touching him in such an intimate way. Or maybe he wasn't thinking of the process as that personal. After all, it was only his hand and female nurses did this type of aid to male patients on a daily basis. However, Tallulah found sliding her fingers over Jim's skin and cradling his hand in her palm to be an erotic experience. So much so that she was finding it hard to keep her breathing on an even keel and her heart from racing.

After smoothing the last piece of tape across the back of his hand, she looked up at him. "All finished. That should keep you clean and covered for a while."

"Thanks," he said. "It feels much better now."

"You're welcome."

She released the gentle hold she had on his fingers, but he didn't step back from her. Instead, he continued to stand close, while his blue eyes made a keen inspection of her face.

Tallulah wondered if he had any idea how much he was affecting her. If he somehow knew that her heart was banging wildly against her ribs and her hands were itching to touch him in all the ways a woman could touch a man.

Finally, he said, "I hope you don't think I invited you over here just to get my hand dressed again."

Her smile felt wobbly. "It never crossed my mind. And anyway, I wouldn't have cared if you had. I want to help you."

Her heart kicked into a faster gear as he lifted his uninjured hand and pushed the fingertips into the hair lying against the side of her neck.

"You have. In more ways than you think."

Once again his gaze fell to her lips, and Tallulah had a real struggle to keep from stepping close enough to press the front of her body against his.

"I haven't really done anything—except clean your kitchen and bandage your hand."

His eyes suddenly took on a soft glow as his gaze roamed her face. "You've lifted my spirits. And reminded me not to feel sorry for myself. That's plenty in my book."

Something in the middle of her chest suddenly turned soft and warm, and it was all she could do to keep from stepping forward and wrapping her arms around him.

"I'm glad," she said softly.

His fingers moved ever so gently in her hair, and her breath caught in her throat as she saw his lashes lower and his head bend slightly toward hers. Then just when she was certain he was going to kiss her, he cleared his throat and eased a step back from her.

"I…uh…imagine our food is getting cold. We'd better go eat."

"Yes, we'd better," she replied. Before she decided to do something reckless and show him just how much she wanted him.

Minutes later, as they ate, Jim inwardly marveled over the fact that he'd found enough strength to exit the bathroom without drawing her into his arms and kissing her over and over.

While she'd been gently administering to his hand, all sorts of thoughts and desires had made dizzying circles in his head. By the time she'd finished smoothing the last piece of tape into place, he'd been aching to taste her lips and feel the softness of her body melding against his.

Jim didn't understand how or why this attraction he felt for Tallulah had developed so rapidly. He only knew that it scared him. He'd never been an impulsive man. The choices he'd made concerning his happiness and future welfare had always been carefully thought through. But this thinking he was doing about Tallulah was far from careful. It was downright reckless. And yet he'd not felt this alive in years and he didn't want to turn back, to hide his emotions behind a sad wall of memories.

"If I finish the last of the dumplings on my plate, I'll be too stuffed for dessert," Tallulah said as she placed her fork on her plate. "And Sophia made blackberry cobbler. The kind with real crust and gobs of cinnamon and sugar on top. It's loaded with calories, but it's one of Maureen's favorites. I honestly don't know how the woman keeps her svelte figure."

"I do. It's all the hard work she puts in from sunup to sundown. She's rarely out of the saddle, and if she is on the ground, she's most likely punching cows into a squeeze chute, or lifting a branding iron."

"Yes, that was one of the first things I noticed about my employer when I moved to the ranch. She's an incredible woman in more ways than one," Tallulah said. "I wish I could be a bit more like her."

The wistful note in her voice had Jim studying her face. "In what way?" he asked.

"She's so strong both emotionally and physically. That's to be admired. But I think…well, I wish I could make wise choices like she's obviously made. She has an adoring husband, children and grandchildren. Even without her money, she'd be a rich woman. And I think she'd be the first to agree with that."

Her remarks didn't surprise Jim. She was the family type. She was the kind of woman who'd relish holding a baby to her breast. She'd want a home and everything that went with it. And yet for now, he didn't want to think about her needs. He didn't even want to stop and consider his own. He merely wanted them to be together without dwelling on the past or future.

"So that's what you'd like for yourself?" he asked. "A husband and kids?"

She let out a long breath before her gaze finally landed on his face.

"Sounds unreasonable, doesn't it? I mean, I married a man who couldn't have been further from the homey type. At the time I was too ignorant or blinded to see that Shane was all about himself. But I'm still fool enough to carry the dream of having a family. So to answer your question, yes. I'd like that…someday. If the right man comes into my life. But for now…well, I want to be careful. I want to make those wise choices I was talking about a moment ago. Instead of jumping blindly into something that will only end up hurting me."

"That's good," he said, then seeing the questioning look on her face, he added, "That you want to be careful. You deserve to be happy the second time around."

A faint smile tilted her lips. "Thank you, Jim. I think you deserve to be happy, too. And to be honest, I've been wondering what you want for yourself—and your future."

Up until he'd met Tallulah a few days ago, Jim

had decided he had everything he wanted. A decent house to live in and a job that he loved. His salary kept him financially secure, and he was surrounded with friends who'd be only too glad to help him if he should need it. What more could a man need to make him happy? Why had he suddenly started thinking about things that he'd lived without for so many years?

Because, like Holt said, it might be nice to have a woman lying next to you at night. It might make you happy to have someone to love. And it would probably be very rewarding to have a child of your own and watch him or her grow into a strong, responsible person. That might be why you've started thinking about Tallulah and all the things she could bring to your life.

The voice in his head sent a cool chill of fear crawling down his back. He'd tried to love before. He'd tried to be a husband and father. But everything had been taken away from him. He'd be crazy to take such a risk for a second time.

"I don't know, Tallulah. What does a man want when he already has what he needs?"

Her brows arched faintly upward. "I can't answer your question. All I know for sure is that a man who quits dreaming and wanting is already dead."

Her thoughtful remark made him inwardly wince, but he did his best not to let her see she'd touched a sore spot.

"Well, let's see. There are a few things I want. Like new rowels for my spurs. And my pocket-knife has a broken blade, so I need to replace it."

When she leveled her warm brown eyes on him, Jim figured she was going to remind him that those were material things and those didn't count as life's dreams. But she didn't. Instead, she gave him a clever little smile.

"You're a cowboy through and through, Jim."

"Does that disappoint you?"

"Not in the least."

She rose to her feet and walked over to the cabinets. Jim couldn't keep his gaze off the soft fabric of her beige skirt and how it clung to her hips and swayed against her calves with each movement she made.

"So do your wants include blackberry cobbler?" she asked as she spooned coffee grounds into the brewing basket.

Not bothering to answer, he left his chair and walked over to where she was filling the glass carafe with cold water.

With her back to him, she didn't realize how close he was until he slipped his arms around her waist and pulled her back against him.

With a little cry of surprise, she set the carafe in the bottom of the sink and turned toward him.

"What—"

He didn't give her a chance to finish. "I thought

I'd show you what I'm wanting—right now, right here."

Her lips parted in question, but his answer didn't come in the form of words. Without hesitation, he drew her tight against him and covered her lips with his.

The sweetness of her lips tasted incredibly wonderful, and her soft curves seemed to melt against him. In a matter of a few brief seconds the kiss went from a gentle exploration to a fiery explosion, and the next thing he knew their tongues were wrapped together in an erotic mating dance, while her arms were curling tightly around his neck.

Hot desire shot straight to his loins and caused his manhood to harden against the fly of his jeans. A roaring sound engulfed his head, and inside his chest, his heart mimicked a sledgehammer as it pounded fiercely against his ribs.

On and on the heated embrace continued until he recognized the sounds in his ears were her moans, and the pressure behind the fly of his jeans was being intensified by the wanton grinding of her hips against his.

The pleasures rocking his body were recklessly pushing him to the edge of a cliff. And he knew with all certainty that if he didn't end the kiss in the next few seconds, they'd end up making love on the floor.

The wild thought was enough to make Jim ease

his mouth from hers, but it wasn't enough to make him step completely away from her. Instead, he rested his head against her forehead and drew in deep, ragged breaths.

"Tallulah, we…uh…need to put on the brakes. Don't you think?"

His voice sounded oddly hoarse and Jim wondered if he'd actually spoken, or if the voice he'd heard was merely his thoughts making a noise in his head.

"Why?"

Her one-word response made him groan. "Because this is…all going too fast. I wouldn't want you to wake up tomorrow and have regrets."

She spoke in a breathless rush. "If I thought I'd have regrets, I wouldn't be standing here with my arms around you."

The knowledge that she might be willing to make love to him was mind-blowing. Yet at the same time he was terrified. Having Tallulah in his bed wouldn't be casual sex. It wouldn't be sex at all. An intimate connection with her would be emotional on so many levels. And he wasn't ready to give her that much of himself. And even if he was ready, was there anything left in him to give?

Chapter Seven

The moment Jim dropped his hold and stepped back from her, Tallulah was forced to reach behind her and grip the edge of the counter for support. At some point during their fiery kiss, the bones in her legs had turned to sand and were now threatening to collapse. Her lungs couldn't work fast enough to satisfy her oxygen-starved body.

Beneath the partial veil of her lashes, she watched Jim thrust a hand through his thick, tawny hair, then wearily swipe the same hand over his face.

Eventually, she was able to speak. "Having regrets, Jim?"

His expression sheepish, he met her gaze. "I was thinking I would. Especially if I didn't stop and allow both of us the time to consider the consequences."

How much time did he think they needed to recognize that the red-hot craving that had sparked between them was something out of the ordinary? Something a person didn't often encounter? Tallulah had kissed other men before her marriage to Shane and after her divorce. But none of those connections came close to the exploding desire she felt when her lips were on Jim's and their arms were around each other.

"You believe the consequences of what we just experienced would be bad? Well, I don't." Her keen gaze took in his tight lips and clamped jaw. "But I guess you weren't seeing stars and hearing birds singing."

His eyes widened as his brows shot straight up. "Were you?"

The question very nearly caused her to groan with frustration, but the odd look on his face caused her to tamp back the sound. He honestly hadn't recognized the depth of her desire, and the idea had Tallulah suddenly seeing him from a totally different view. Yes, he was a widower and his wife's death had clearly altered his life. But she had the feeling his reticence about making love was not entirely about the loss of his late wife, but more of a lack of experience with women. Which was hardly a bad thing. It was just something she'd never dealt with before.

"Yes. I was seeing stars and hearing birds," she

said softly, then feeling a bit embarrassed for admitting it, she turned back to the sink. "I'll make that coffee now. Before the cobbler gets cold."

As she filled the carafe with tap water, she heard his step and then felt his hand rest on the back of her shoulder. The touch was warm and had her body longing to turn and repeat the heated kiss they'd just shared. But why would she want to? All her kiss was doing to him was filling him with regrets.

"I'm sorry, Tallulah."

"Don't be sorry," she said bluntly. "There's nothing to be sorry for."

"Yes. There is. I started all of this and then I stopped—just when things were getting…"

When he didn't go on, she finished for him. "Hot?"

"Yeah," he muttered as though he was guilty of committing a crime. "Now you're taking it personally and—"

This time she couldn't stop the short laugh that escaped her lips. "Personally? Oh Lord, Jim, how much more personal could it be? You were kissing me!"

His fingers tightened on the flesh of her shoulder, and then she felt his bandaged hand come to rest on the opposite shoulder. And suddenly, the knowledge that he wanted to touch her, even though it might cause him pain, turned everything inside her to a helpless muddle.

"You think I don't know that?" he grunted ruefully. "Tallulah, you're not just a woman I met sitting on the barstool next to mine!"

"There's nothing wrong with a woman sitting in a bar. Or a man meeting her there," Tallulah told him.

He let out a long sigh. "I didn't say there was. I only meant that...well, I don't want to treat you like a one-night stand."

"I'm not sure you want to treat me as a long-term girlfriend, either," she said flatly. "But that's okay, Jim. A couple of kisses hardly binds us together. I understand."

"How could you? I can't explain any of this to myself." He tugged her around to face him. "Come with me to the living room. I want to show you something."

She glanced over her shoulder at the glass carafe. She'd already made two attempts to get the coffee brewing. She supposed it hardly mattered if she had to make a third.

Following the direction of her gaze, he said, "We'll do dessert later. This is more important."

"All right," she told him.

They walked out to the living room, and he gestured toward the couch where Georgette was curled up on an end cushion.

"Have a seat," he said.

He went over to the fireplace mantel and picked up a framed picture. Tallulah sat down on the cushion next to the cat and waited for him to join her.

With the photo in hand, he eased down next to her. "I should've shown this to you before now," he said solemnly. "I…uh…I'm not very good at explaining things. Especially something about myself."

He angled the wood frame so she could have a full view of the enlarged snapshot, and Tallulah curiously studied the outdoor scene of a young woman. She appeared to be quite a bit taller than Tallulah and very slender. She was dressed in jeans and a black tank top. Her blondish-brown hair was parted down the middle of her head and hung straight all the way to her waist. A wide smile was on her pretty face, but it was impossible to know whether the happy expression was meant for the photographer or the bay horse hanging his head over her shoulder.

"That's my late wife, Lyndsey. The picture was taken a few months before the accident. She was about to turn twenty-five when she died."

There was a hollowness to his voice, like an empty echo traveling through a desolate canyon. Tallulah hated the sound.

She glanced at him. "How old were you at that time?"

"Twenty-nine. We'd been married about three years."

Tallulah swallowed as a lump of emotion collected in her throat. She'd thought losing a spouse through divorce was bad, and it had been. But what she'd gone through with Shane couldn't compare to Jim's loss.

"She was very pretty. Was she a horsewoman?"

"An excellent horsewoman. She'd been racing barrels since she was about eight years old. Later, in her teens, she began training horses for barrel competition. After we married she took a job doing office work for a construction company and continued to train horses in her off-hours."

"Sounds like horses were important to her."

"Yeah. They were the common denominator that brought us together. She never made much money off her training, but the business was beginning to grow and she was proud of her little successes. I was proud for her."

Tallulah's gaze traveled over to his strong profile, and as she took in his somber expression, she wondered what kind of man he'd been back then. Had Lyndsey's love kept him happy and smiling? Had he been an attentive and supporting husband? So many questions about him were rifling through her mind, yet she understood she needed to be cautious about how and when she asked him about that personal part of his life.

"You mentioned she had an accident. Was it a car wreck?"

He blew out a long breath. "A car wreck probably would have been easier to understand. But no, Lyndsey was fatally injured by a horse. It happened at a rodeo in northern California. She'd gone to watch a friend run barrels on a horse that Lyndsey had trained. The heck of it, I had felt uneasy about her going and tried to talk her out of it."

"You didn't make the trip with her?"

His expression grim, he shook his head. "It was during a busy time at the track. I couldn't get away. So to ease my worries, Lyndsey talked her mother into making the trip with her." He paused and drew in a deep breath. "Unfortunately, her mother ended up seeing the accident that caused her daughter to lose her life."

Tallulah was horrified at the thought. "Oh, the poor woman. That's unthinkable! But I don't understand, Jim. Why was Lyndsey riding her friend's horse? To warm it up for her, or something?"

"She wasn't riding the horse," he said grimly. "She was helping her saddle the animal when pyrotechnics used in a clown act exploded out in the arena. The commotion startled the horse and it reared up and fell over sideways to the ground, taking Lyndsey with him. The horse was unharmed, but my wife wasn't so fortunate."

"Oh. Such a horrible thing to have happened."

He swiped a hand over his face. "Yeah. I was stunned. But later…well, I realized, as well as anyone who's ever dealt with horses, that weird and unexpected things can happen. I just never could understand why it had to happen to her."

"It's human nature to wonder why things happen," she said.

He shrugged. "Since the accident I've tried to forget and move forward. Most of the time I don't dwell on losing Lyndsey. But there are times— like tonight—when it all comes back to mess with my mind."

At least it was his mind and not his heart that was getting mixed up, Tallulah thought.

"Are you telling me that you feel guilty about kissing me?" she asked softly. "You believe that somehow you're being disloyal to your late wife?"

"No. Not guilty or disloyal. I feel—" He broke off with a frustrated groan. "It's hard to explain, Tallulah. A doomed notion comes over me, and I get to thinking if I let myself care again, then I'll only end up losing again."

He was afraid to risk his heart a second time. Oh yes, Tallulah could understand his fear. For the longest time after her divorce, she'd believed the best thing she could do for herself would be to remain single for the rest of her life. But as time had taken away some of the pain, she'd come to realize that hiding behind her disappointments would be the same as hiding from life.

Tallulah reached over and settled her hand on his knee. "To be honest, Jim, there are times I feel the same way. Handing your heart over to someone isn't an easy thing to do. For a long time after my split with Shane, I swore I'd never open myself up to that kind of pain again. But I finally realized that life is too wonderful to miss any part of it. True, I might never meet a man I'll want to make a family with, but I don't intend to give up trying."

Long moments passed as his blue eyes delved into hers, and then finally his gaze dropped to the photograph of Lyndsey. "Now you're probably thinking I should put this constant reminder of the past where I can't see it."

Her fingers tightened ever so slightly on his knee. "No. I think it would be far better if you could look at the image of your late wife and be able to say to yourself that that was then and this is now. And you're not going to let the past ruin your future."

"Easy to say. Hard to do."

Rising from the couch, he walked over and replaced the photo on the mantelpiece. When he returned to his seat at her side, he reached for her hand and Tallulah was only too happy to allow his fingers to slide between hers.

"Tell me, can you look at a picture of your ex-husband and put all of the disappointment behind you?"

The contact of his hand wrapped intimately around hers was causing an upheaval with her senses, but she did her best not to let him see or guess the enormous impact his touch had on her. He wasn't ready for passion to flare between them. Or so he said. But what was she supposed to do? Go home and take cold showers?

"It bothers me much more to look at myself in those old photos," she admitted wryly. "Because I see a fool who'd trusted too much. Who'd been blinded by too many stars in her eyes. But I keep trying to assure myself that I've grown and learned since then. At least, I hope I have."

Shifting toward him, she met his gaze head-on. "Jim, are you thinking you'd rather not be with me anymore? If that's how you really feel, then I'll honor your wishes and keep my distance."

Clearly amazed by her suggestion, he stared at her. "Are you joking? After that kiss we just had in the kitchen, you honestly think I don't want to be with you?"

She frowned. "Well, you didn't exactly keep on kissing me," she said in an attempt to explain.

His features softened as he pulled his hand from hers and thrust his fingers into her hair. Stroking the silky strands away from her cheek, he gave her a wry smile. "If you really want to know why

I stopped, it was because I was seeing stars and hearing birds, too. And I knew if we continued on, we were going to end up in the bedroom."

The mere thought of sharing Jim's bed made her heart thump hard and fast. "And you don't want that to happen," she stated matter-of-factly.

He shook his head with misgivings. "I do. But not until I'm sure I can give you what you want— what both of us want."

She didn't know exactly what he meant by that, but just hearing him admit he wanted to make love to her was enough to give her a glimmer of hope for the two of them.

Smiling gently, she reached up and touched her fingertips to his face. "I don't want to scare you off, Jim. I don't want you to be afraid that I could ever hurt you. I wouldn't. Not for anything."

"Oh, Tallulah." The hand in her hair slipped to the back of her head and drew her face forward until his lips were hovering close to hers. "I never thought anything like this would happen to me. I don't want to give up this feeling I have when I'm with you. But I think we need to slow down a bit. I want us both to take the time to think about everything—first."

She moved her head just close enough for her lips to brush his as she spoke. "You mean instead of just feeling how good it is to be in your arms and having your lips on mine?"

"You're not playing fair," he said with a groan, then closed the last fraction of space between their lips.

He kissed her just long enough to stir up a wave of longing deep within her, and then he drew back and caressed her cheek with his fingers.

"I think it's time we go dig into the cobbler," he said. "What do you think?"

Before Tallulah could agree, Georgette let out a loud meow. They both looked down to see the orange tabby sitting on the floor in front of the couch, staring impatiently up at them.

Smiling, Tallulah said, "I think Georgette's answer is yes."

Chuckling, Jim drew Tallulah to her feet and as the two of them walked to the kitchen, the cat followed close on their heels.

Four days later Tallulah decided to use the afternoon hours before the children came home from school to make a trip into town to do a bit of shopping for herself. Taking little Madison with her, she'd made a few stops at a couple of boutiques and a small discount store before she eventually drove over to Conchita's, a coffee shop operated by her sister-in-law, Emily-Ann.

The weather was hot and sunny, but both women chose to sit outside at one of the wrought-iron tables, rather than coop up in the tiny air-conditioned building. Especially since the outdoor sitting area was shaded by the branches of two huge mesquite trees.

"I stopped on the chance that you might not be busy," Tallulah said to Emily-Ann as she carefully placed Madison in the chair next to hers.

"I'm so glad you did. We don't get to see each other often enough. And midafternoon is always slow here at the shop. Sometimes I have a few stragglers, and those usually want iced coffee. But I've not had a customer at all in the past half hour."

The tall redhead set her nineteen-month-old son, Brody, on a grassy patch of ground near the table and to keep him occupied, placed several miniature trucks and tractors within his reach.

"If you can watch both kids, I'll go get our drinks," she said to Tallulah. "Let's see, you want French roast with lots of cream and sugar. And, unfortunately, I want anything without calories. Brody just drank a glass of milk, so he's full. What about Madison?"

Hearing her name mentioned, the girl pointed to Brody and shouted eagerly, "Brody. Me play, too, Nanneee!"

"Looks like she's going to be too busy playing with your son to drink anything," Tallulah told Emily-Ann. "You go on and get our coffee. I'll deal with the kids."

Nodding, Emily-Ann left to go fetch their drinks.

Tallulah picked up the little girl and placed her on the ground next to Brody. Before they'd left the ranch house, Tallulah had dressed the child in cotton shorts and a matching top. Hopefully, if she got grass stains on her clothing, they would wash out in the laundry.

"Okay, Maddie, you can play with Brody. But you have to stay right here with him. Remember to play gentle. He's not as old as you are, and you wouldn't want to make him cry. So be nice."

"Me nice! Nice! Nice!" Madison cried out in a happy singsong voice.

Emily-Ann laughed as she approached the table with two large red coffee mugs in hand. "I'll say one thing, Tallulah. You're a dedicated nanny. You get a few hours off in the afternoons to do whatever you'd like and today you bring Jazelle's daughter to town with you on a shopping trip."

Tallulah sank into one of the chairs at the table. "Madison is a joy. And she doesn't get to do all the things the older kids do, so I wanted to give her a special treat today. Actually, she's been a good girl this whole afternoon."

"You need to give me childcare lessons," her sister-in-law joked as she took a seat across from Tallulah. "If I took Brody into a boutique, I'd probably owe thousands of dollars in damages before I had a chance to turn around."

Tallulah laughed. "Oh, come on, my little nephew isn't that naughty."

Emily-Ann rolled her eyes in a good-natured way. "Of course he isn't. Not when he's around you. I think you must put some sort of good behavior spell over kids. Is that your secret?"

"Patience is my secret." She chuckled, then took an appreciative sip of coffee before asking, "So what's been going on with you? When I talked to Tag on the phone yesterday, he mentioned that you'd heard about a nursing position opening at the clinic. He doesn't think you want to apply for it, though. Is that right?"

Emily-Ann nodded as she used her forefinger to draw abstract shapes on the tabletop. "The position is open and it would be an easy one. But honestly, Tallulah, I don't want to leave Brody. And I love running the coffee shop. I've had this job for so long that I'd miss seeing all the regulars and my friends who stop by to say hello and chat over a pastry. I guess that sounds so unambitious to you, but it's just me and I can't change me. Someday I'll put my nursing education to use. But for now, Tag and I want a bigger family, so I want to put all my focus on that."

Tallulah thoughtfully studied her sister-in-law. "You worked hard to acquire your nursing degree. I'm proud of you for that, and I know you have to be proud of yourself. But listen, I'm the last person to be telling you the sort of career you need. I chose chasing after kids instead of a desk job. So I say, you should do what makes *you* happy."

Emily-Ann shot her a grateful smile. "That's what Tag tells me, too. You know, I'm so lucky to be married to your brother. He lets me be me. And speaking of marriages, I heard from Camille yesterday. She said her, Matt and baby Harry are coming up for Colt and Sophia's wedding in June. I was happy to get the news. What with Matt working so hard to build up Red Bluff and Camille running the diner, I wasn't sure if they'd be able to take time off to make the trip."

Tallulah had only met Camille one time, and that had been shortly after she'd taken the nanny job. The youngest Hollister sibling and her husband had made a one-night trip to Three Rivers in order to pick up a seed bull. Camille had been an especially lovely woman, and Tallulah had liked her immediately.

"I'm happy to hear they'll be visiting the ranch," Tallulah told her. "Camille seemed very down to earth and fun. It's easy to see why the two of you have been good friends since your childhood days."

"We'll always be close, even though she lives a few hundred miles away," Emily-Ann said.

"You're fortunate," Tallulah replied. "I don't have a close friend. Not like you and Camille. I had plenty of friends during my school days, but after we grew up we all drifted apart."

Emily-Ann gave her a bright smile. "Now that you've moved to Arizona you're making new friends," she remarked, then steered the conversation back to Sophia and Colt's wedding. "I'm hearing that Maureen is going all-out on this one. But then Maureen doesn't do any celebration just halfway. And I think she wants to make it extra special for Reeva's sake."

Tallulah nodded. "I've not been at Three Rivers long enough to see any of her big parties. But I've heard about them."

Emily-Ann chuckled. "You're in for an experience. Frankly, I can't wait to see what she's planning for the occasion. I imagine there will be slews of flowers and candles and food and music. Oh, and champagne. I shouldn't forget the fancy bubbly."

It always lifted Tallulah's spirits to spend time with her sister-in-law. Emily-Ann was a genuinely happy person, and she'd made Tallulah's brother happier than she'd ever seen him. Which was quite a turnaround from the somber guy who'd considered his life over when he'd lost his young wife and unborn baby in a car accident back in Texas.

Ever since Jim had shown Tallulah the picture of his wife and explained how the woman had died, she'd been thinking how eerily similar his tragic past was to Taggart's. As for her brother, Tallulah had feared he would never allow himself to love or marry again. But Emily-Ann had changed him. Now Tallulah could only wonder if she could possibly chase the cold shadows from Jim's heart and make him want to try love again. Or was that idea as foolish as her believing Shane had wanted to be a real family man?

"Emily-Ann, tell me, how did you ever get Tag to thinking about love and marriage?" Tallulah asked as she thoughtfully stirred her coffee. "To be honest, I was afraid he'd remain single for the rest of his life."

Shaking her head, Emily-Ann rolled her eyes toward the blue sky. "Oh, your brother and I had a rocky romance. First of all, I didn't think I was good enough to be Tag's wife. I came from a poor background, and Tag is so handsome and successful at what he does. I felt darned intimidated. Actually, I couldn't believe he even looked at me in the first place. I'm not exactly a raving beauty."

Emily-Ann was tall and curvy with gorgeous auburn hair that hung to her waist. The clothes she wore were uniquely retro, and to Tallulah she always looked feminine and attractive. "Don't be silly. You're beautiful. That's why Tag gave you a first and second and third look," she said with a pointed grin.

Emily-Ann took a drink from her mug before

she replied. "Well, when I first met your brother I guess my self-esteem was kind of low. And then Tag was carrying all those painful memories of his late wife and child. Getting the two of us together was a real tussle."

Tallulah absently rubbed her finger along the handle of the coffee mug. "I don't know if Tag has mentioned this to you, but I've been spending a bit of time with Jim Garroway."

Emily-Ann nodded. "Yes. He told me he'd called and talked to you about Jim. I hope you didn't get cross with him for butting in."

"I'd never get cross with Tag. He's always been overly protective of me. Anyway, I assured my brother that I wasn't jumping into anything too quickly."

Emily-Ann's expression turned skeptical. "You're not? Jazelle tells me you've been going over to his place every night," she said, then quickly pressed a hand over her mouth. "Oh, sorry. I'm gossiping. And now you're going to be angry at Jazelle for talking to me about you."

From the corner of her eye, Tallulah watched Madison pluck a hand full of grass and dump it over Brody's head. The toddler squealed with delight and rubbed both his hands over the top of his curly red hair. The sight of the children's happy play struck a melancholy chord in Tallulah, and suddenly the fear that she might never have children of her own struck her hard.

"Tallulah? Oh Lord, now you're angry at me. I'm sorry. I'm always running off at the mouth and saying things I shouldn't be saying."

Blinking her eyes, Tallulah looked over at her sister-in-law's remorseful face.

"Oh, I'm not angry. And I don't care one whit that Jazelle told you about me and Jim. I was… uh…thinking about something else."

Emily-Ann let out a sigh of relief. "Thank goodness. For a minute there I thought you were going to cry." Leaning over the tabletop, she peered worriedly at Tallulah. "You aren't, are you?"

"No! I'm fine. Really."

She flashed her a wide smile. "Good. Then back to you and Jim. Is he someone you think you could get serious about? Or is it just a casual type thing?"

Tallulah shrugged. "He's a hot hunk of man. And he's also incredibly nice and kind. But…"

Emily-Ann motioned for her to continue. "But what?"

"Okay. He's just like Tag used to be. He's a widower and can't get past his wife's death. I'm beginning to get the weird feeling that whenever I'm with him, her ghost is sitting between us."

Or whenever he was kissing her, the memory of his late wife was whirling around in his head, she thought miserably. How could she ever expect to deal with such an intangible rival?

Emily-Ann said, "Oh, you poor thing."

"Right," Tallulah said glumly. "I thought you might have some advice for me. Since you went through the same thing with Tag."

"I'm not so sure about advice, Tallulah. Except that I finally lost all patience with Tag. And I grew angry with myself for waiting around on him to wake up and see the present instead of the past. I finally told him it was over between us, and I meant it. But then I discovered I was pregnant and that complicated everything."

There was certainly no danger of her getting pregnant, Tallulah thought. For the past four nights she'd taken supper over to Jim's house, and during each of those evenings, they'd ended up sharing some heated kisses. But each time Jim had ended up pulling away from her, and Tallulah was beginning to wonder if she was wasting her time.

Not that having sex with the man was so crucial at this point in their relationship. It wasn't. Tallulah would be happy to wait until he felt things were right between them. But each time he'd kissed her, she could feel his restraint. Which told her one of two things. He either wanted her so much he was having to fight to keep from making love to her. Or he was struggling because deep down he was a good and decent guy and he couldn't see their relationship develop into anything serious.

"You shouldn't worry," her sister-in-law continued. "If you really like the guy and he's honestly into you, then everything will eventually work out. I'm not going to say it will be easy. God knows it wasn't easy for Tag and I. But in the end it's all worth it. I don't have to tell you how happy we are. You can see it for yourself."

Closing her eyes, Tallulah wearily pinched the bridge of her nose. "Yes, I can see. And I'm so happy for you and Tag. But I had such hopes when I married Shane. And nothing about our marriage turned out right or good. I'm afraid to hope with Jim. And yet I can't help myself. I want to believe that he might…"

"Fall in love with you? Want a life with you?" Her expression full of empathy, Emily-Ann reached across the small table and patted the back of Tallulah's hand. "That's what happens when a woman falls in love. She can't help but hope."

Tallulah's eyes flew open and so did her mouth. "It hasn't been that long since I first met the guy. I couldn't be in love with Jim!"

Her smile knowing, Emily-Ann made a palm's up gesture. "Really? Then you don't have a thing to worry about."

"No. Not a thing." Tallulah picked up her coffee, and after gulping down the last few swallows, she rose to her feet. "I'd better get Madison and head back to the ranch. It's not that long until I pick up the kids at the school-bus stop."

Emily-Ann glanced at her watch. "Yikes, it's almost closing time for me, too."

Tallulah scooped up Madison from her play spot on the ground, a move that caused Brody to burst into tears and reach beseechingly up to the little girl.

"Maddee, Mama! Maddee!"

Emily-Ann cast a look of helpless humor over at Tallulah before she reached down and gathered the toddler into her arms.

Kissing the boy's tearstained cheek, she attempted to soothe him. "It's okay, son. Maddie has to go bye-bye. But we'll see her soon. And right now, we have to go home and get ready to see Daddy."

As soon as she spoke the word *Daddy*, Brody looked up at her in wonder and then a slobbery grin spread over his face.

"Da-Da! Da-Da!"

Tallulah smiled. "I think you said the magic word."

Emily-Ann chuckled. "It usually does the trick."

She walked over and pressed a light kiss to Tallulah's cheek. "I'm so glad you stopped by. Maybe the two of us can do something together soon. Like a day of shopping in Phoenix. Come to think of it, we might need new dresses to wear to Sophia's wedding."

"Yes. A perfect reason for a shopping trip." Tallulah gave her sister-in-law a brief hug, then pecked a kiss on Brody's cheek. "Thanks for the coffee. We'll talk soon, okay?"

"Sure. And I have a feeling that Jim is going to open his eyes and see you instead of his late wife."

Tallulah only wished she could feel as positive as Emily-Ann, but presently her spirits were slumping.

"See ya." She gave her sister-in-law and nephew a little wave and then carried Madison out to the SUV.

After strapping the girl safely into the child car seat, she started the engine and was about to drive onto the main street when her cell phone rang.

Pressing on the brake, she stopped the car in the empty parking lot and reached for the phone lying in a tray on the console.

When she saw that the caller was Jim, her heart took off in a mad dash.

"Hello, Jim."

"Hi, Tallulah. Are you busy?"

Like she could ever be too busy to talk to him? She suddenly felt so bubbly inside it was all she could do to keep from laughing.

"Not at all. Actually, I'm in Wickenburg. I just had coffee with Emily-Ann at Conchita's."

"That's good. The reason I'm calling is to see if you're still planning to come over tonight."

Her brows pulled slightly together. Was he going to say he had something else to do? If so, she was going to be disappointed. Which would be silly of her. She'd spent every evening this week with the man. He might be needing some private time of his own.

"Yes, I was planning on bringing supper over. Unless you have other plans. If you do, that's okay. You're probably getting tired of my company anyway."

A stretch of silence followed her response, while in the background she caught the sound of horses nickering, metal gates clanging and cowboys yelling to each other. He was obviously calling from the horse barn, she decided.

Finally, he said, "Actually, I thought it might be nice if we went out somewhere tonight."

The mad dash her heart had taken earlier now changed into a series of cartwheels. "We? As in the two of us?"

He chuckled. "Well, yes. Unless there's someone else you'd like to bring along with us."

Realizing how inane she must have sounded, she laughed. "Oh…uh, no! You caught me off guard, that's all. The two of us going out together sounds great."

"I'm glad you think so. Will you be over about the same time?"

"Yes. Unless something unforeseen comes up. If it does, I'll text you."

"Okay. I—" He broke off as a loud commotion sounded nearby, then said in a sudden rush, "Uh, sorry—I gotta go. Farley is just asking to be pawed in the head! See you later!"

The connection went dead, but the abrupt end to their conversation was hardly enough to stem Tallulah's excitement.

Grinning from ear to ear, she put the phone away and glanced around at Madison. The girl was clapping her hands together as if she'd already guessed Tallulah was happy.

"Yippee, Maddie! Nanny is going on a date!"

"Date! Yay! Yay! Nanneee! Me go, too!"

Tallulah chuckled as she steered the vehicle onto the street. "Not this time, Maddie."

Tonight she wanted Jim to focus solely on her and not the woman he was trying to forget.

Chapter Eight

Something had happened to Jim since Rowdy had thrown a kicking fit six days ago and smashed his hand against the wall of the stall. Sure, he'd learned it was hell trying to work with only one good hand and even harder trying to hide the excruciating pain from Holt and the other men.

However, the changes he'd experienced after the injury were far more than physical. The night he'd shown Tallulah the snapshot of Lyndsey and explained how she'd died, something inside him had snapped and the tight rein he'd held over his emotions had gone slack. All of a sudden he'd begun to feel things he'd not felt in years. Moreover, he'd begun to see Tallulah in a whole new way.

She was a lovely, caring woman and he wanted to be with her. He wanted the sunshine in her smile and the warmth of her touch. If that meant he'd

gone a little crazy, he couldn't help it. If that meant
he was headed for heartache, then so be it. At least,
he was beginning to feel like a whole man again.

Now Jim stood at the vanity in the bathroom
and fumbled with a strip of adhesive tape on the
back of his hand. Tallulah was probably going to
take one look at his clumsy effort and insist she
do the bandage over. But tonight he'd wanted to
give her a break and take care of the task himself.
Hopefully by the time she spotted the lopsided
gauze and sagging tape, the two of them would
already be away from the house and on their way
to dinner.

Satisfied that he'd done the best he could do
with the bandage, he went to his bedroom and
pulled on his jeans and shirt. As he snapped the
rust-red shirt over his chest, he noticed Georgette
had entered the room and was sitting back on her
haunches, staring up at him.

"Yep, Georgie, I'm going out tonight. What do
you think? That I've gone a little off the beam? Or
you think I'm getting wiser?"

The cat meowed while Jim leaned closer to the
dresser mirror and peered at his image. He didn't
understand what Tallulah saw in him. He wasn't
a handsome man. Not like Holt or the Crawford
brothers. He didn't even have the charm of young
and innocent Farley. Yet when she looked at Jim,
he could see attraction, even admiration in her

eyes, and the sight never failed to knock him for a little loop. It also made him feel a bit guilty.

Tallulah had made it clear from the start that she wanted marriage and children to be a part of her future. Even though he'd felt a change come over him, he'd not experienced enough of a transformation to give him dreams of being a husband and father again. Especially when the mere thought of Tallulah being pregnant with his child sent a chill down his spine.

Yes, having a child with her would be a blessing beyond belief. But he, more than anyone, knew that anything could go wrong. Who could assure him that he wouldn't lose a second wife? Or a second child?

No, sooner or later he was going to have to give her up so that she'd be free to find a man who'd love her completely. A man who'd be glad to give her children and make a home with her. But for the present, he didn't want to think about Tallulah loving another man. He wanted to hold on to the pleasure of pretending she would always be at his side.

Jim had just finished pulling on his boots and buckling his belt when he heard Tallulah's knock announcing her arrival.

When he opened the door to see her standing on the porch, gazing at the view of the bluff, a strange feeling struck him from out of nowhere. And for one brief moment, he stood on the threshold, dumbfounded by the thoughts rushing through his head.

It felt like she belonged here!

Shaken by the odd clairvoyant reaction, Jim cleared his throat and stepped onto the porch to greet her.

"Good evening."

She turned and he held out his arms to her. With a wide smile, she walked straight into his embrace.

"Hello, Jim." She pressed a kiss to his cheek, then with a little laugh, leaned her head back far enough to gaze into his eyes. "You look like a different man tonight."

Jim could've told her he felt like a different man, too. In fact, he wasn't quite sure where this "other man" had come from. He was just glad he'd finally shown up.

Grinning, he asked, "Different as in good or bad?"

"Oh, definitely good."

He kissed her smooth forehead, then resting his hand on her upper arm, ushered her into the house.

In the living room, he gathered up his hat from a wall table and levered it onto his head. "I hope you won't resent racing off like this, but I'd like to get an early start. I had it in mind that we'd drive over to Cave Creek. Have you had a chance to go there yet?"

"No. But I've heard lots about the place from

Jazelle. She and Connor go over there from time to time. She says the drive on Highway 74 is pretty."

She glanced down at her green-and-white-patterned dress. "But I didn't exactly dress for anything fancy tonight. I thought you might be taking me to the Broken Spur."

He let out a hearty laugh. "Oh, Tallulah, you're precious."

She leveled a look of comical confusion at him. "Why are you laughing?"

He walked over and clasped his hands over the tops of her shoulders. "First of all, you look gorgeous. Too gorgeous for a saddle tramp like me. And the idea that you'd be willing to go to a ratty café like the Spur with me is really special. But the notion that you thought I'd be taking you there on our first date is even funnier."

Her brown eyes twinkled and the corners of her soft mouth tilted upward. "This is our first date? It feels like number ten or eleven, or twelve to me."

His hands slipped to her back, which was exposed by a cutout in the bodice of her dress. Her skin was incredibly smooth and warm, and he allowed his fingers to linger there.

"I can't imagine why," he murmured. "We've been here in this house every night this week."

"Yes, but we've been together. And we've been getting to know one another. And we've shared a few…uh, warm kisses. So it sort of feels like we've been dating."

Warm kisses? Holding Tallulah in his arms was like embracing a flaming torch. And the longer he held her, the greater the risk of getting scorched.

"Yeah. It sort of feels that way to me, too."

Uncertainty flickered in her eyes as she slowly searched his face. "Honestly, Jim, until you called me this afternoon, I didn't believe you were thinking of me as your girlfriend."

In the beginning he balked at the idea of becoming connected to Tallulah in a personal way. Not as a girlfriend, or lover, or anything in between. Yet the more time he spent with her, the more she was becoming a part of his life. It would be pointless of him to try to deny the obvious.

"I've been thinking about you in all sorts of ways, Tallulah," he admitted. "And today at work Farley and Riggs asked me if I was dating you. The question made me a little ashamed of myself."

Her lips twisted to a wry slant. "Why? Because your coworkers suggested that we're a couple?"

"Absolutely not! I felt awful because you've been doing so much for me, and I've not bothered to show you any appreciation. Or how much I've come to like you."

She wrapped her arm around his and urged him toward the front door.

He arched a brow at her. "What's wrong? Getting impatient to get to the dinner table?" he asked in a teasing tone.

A suggestive grin curved her lips. "My stomach can wait on dinner. Right now, I think we should get going. Before I change my mind and decide I want to keep you all to myself."

He placed a swift kiss on her mouth, then with his lips hovering above hers, whispered, "Yeah. We'd better leave. Before I change my mind, too."

Jazelle had been right in telling Tallulah the drive over to Cave Creek was a pretty one. On either side of the highway, desert and mountains stretched as far as the eye could see. Along the foothills, saguaros grew tall and thick, while other areas were dotted with thorny chaparral and wispy mesquite trees.

"I'm glad we were able to leave early enough to have a daylight drive," Tallulah told him as he steered the truck along the curving highway. "This is beautiful."

"I'm pleased that you're enjoying the scenery," he said. "That was my main intention. You deserve to have a little break from being my nursemaid all week."

She looked away from the rugged landscape and over to his tanned profile. "Nonsense. I haven't been your nursemaid. All I've done is change your bandage and bring you something to eat." Her gaze dropped to the bandaged hand resting on his thigh. "And from the looks of your bandage tonight, I think you should probably consider taking first-aid lessons. If you're not careful, you might lose that bandage before the night is over."

He chuckled. "Aww, come on, Tallulah, you should give me an A for trying. Especially for a one-handed effort. Anyway, I doubt it would hurt anything if the bandage did fall off. The stitches are all still in place, and the wound appears to be closed."

"When do you have the stitches removed? Or do you plan on doing that task yourself?"

"I would do it myself, but the doctor wants to have a look first. I see him next Tuesday. That's four more days. Hopefully he'll remove them at that time."

"If you get rid of your stitches, then Tuesday will call for a celebration," she declared, then asked, "What happened with Farley after you hung up the phone this afternoon? The situation sounded urgent."

He shook his head in helpless fashion. "It could've turned out worse than urgent," he told her. "Farley started out as a barn worker a little more than a year ago. Since then he's been trying to move up in jobs and become a groom. So he's still green about handling horses. Colt and I are both trying to teach him, but it takes years to learn some things. Farley was trying to lead a yearling down the alleyway of the barn, but the young horse didn't want to go. Farley kept pulling straight forward on the lead rope until the horse began rearing up and pawing the air. A hoof came close to taking a slice out of the kid's head. I had to run and get the horse away from him."

"Oh my. I've heard logging is deemed the most dangerous job, but I think whoever did that research is wrong. It should be changed to working in the horse barn on Three Rivers Ranch."

He chuckled. "There's never a dull moment, Tallulah."

Since she'd learned that his late wife had died from a horse accident, she'd wondered how Jim had been able to continue to work around the animals. Clearly he didn't blame all horses for his wife's death. Which was a good thing, she supposed. Because she could see he loved his job.

"I say that fairly often about my own job," she said with a chuckle. "But thankfully it's not physically dangerous. It's more of a mental challenge. Emily-Ann thinks I'm overly devoted because I had a few hours off today and, instead of going shopping alone, I took Madison with me."

"Because you're comfortable with kids," he said flatly. "Even I can see that."

The slight change in his tone of voice had her thoughtfully glancing at him. His focus remained glued to the highway in front of them, while his expression appeared blank. Perhaps she was imagining things, but it seemed as though whenever she brought up the subject of children, he withdrew to some other place in his mind.

Dear God, she hoped her impression was wrong. It had to be wrong. With her own two eyes, she'd seen how gently he'd treated the children when she'd taken them to the horse barn to see Ranger Red.

Hanging on to that softer image, she said, "Yes. And even I can see you're comfortable with horses."

Grinning at that, he glanced at her and Tallulah felt a sense of relief.

He said, "I think you're beginning to know me."

That's what happens when a woman falls in love.

Emily-Ann's words came to her out of nowhere, and Tallulah suddenly realized that with just the tiniest of nudges, she could fall head over heels in love with Jim. Or maybe she was already falling and hadn't yet realized what was happening? Either way, he'd become important to her. More important than anything else in her life.

"I see town up ahead," he suddenly announced. "I hope you're hungry. There's a restaurant where I've eaten before that I thought you might enjoy."

His words penetrated her churning thoughts,

and she looked out the windshield to see they were swiftly approaching the outskirts of Cave Creek.

"I am hungry," she told him. "And don't worry. If you liked the food, I'm sure I'll love it."

Everything about the little town held a southwestern flavor. The streets were lined with an assortment of shops, boutiques and eating places. Most of the buildings were structured in a frontier style with flat roofs and false board fronts. Others were made of smooth stucco with a few sporting gracefully arched porticos. The entrances and open areas surrounding each business were all landscaped with beautiful desert vegetation, some of which was blooming.

Tallulah was enthralled, and she openly oohed and aahed as Jim drove through a main portion of the business area. When he eventually turned on a northbound street, the business buildings gave way to a countryside of gentle slopes covered with mesquite trees, majestic saguaros and patches of colorful wildflowers.

"Looks like we're leaving town," she said. "Are you sure you're on the right road?"

"I'm sure. The restaurant is just outside of Cave Creek," he explained. "Right over this rise."

Less than five minutes later, Jim parked the truck in a graveled parking area located at the far end of a low rambling building with board siding painted dark brown and trimmed halfway up with natural rock. A long porch sheltered the front entrance while a neon green sign in the window read Pedro's Ranchero.

Inside, they walked through a short foyer decorated with potted succulents and photos of nearby Black Mountain and a local mine where a prospector discovered gold back in 1874.

At the end of the foyer they were met by a young woman with long black hair pulled into a low ponytail and dressed in a yellow peasant blouse with a multicolored striped floor length skirt.

"Would you like to dine inside or outside on the patio?" She directed the question to Jim, then glanced to Tallulah for further affirmation.

Jim looked to Tallulah. "It's beautiful outside on the patio," he said. "I think you'll like it."

"The patio sounds lovely," she told him, while recalling the dinner they'd shared on the patio behind the Three Rivers Ranch house. He'd jumped up and run from her that night. But hopefully, he'd gotten over the urge to run from her now.

The hostess led them through the main area of the restaurant, which was furnished with heavy wooden tables and chairs and decorated with colorful serape blankets pinned to the walls, along with a huge collection of old cowboy memorabilia. Spanish guitar music was playing lowly in the background, while several people dined at the tables.

On the far side of the room, they passed through

a set of glass doors, then stepped onto a large patio area equipped with small square tables made of black iron and topped with Aztec tile. The floor was constructed of intricately laid brick, and in the very center, a circular bench was made of stone and mortar. Huge pots of bunny ear cacti, agave and burros tail sat in random spots around the quiet outdoor space, while strings of small clear lights were draped from the overhanging limbs of mesquite trees.

"You may choose the table you'd like," the hostess told them.

Jim gestured for Tallulah to make the choice, and after taking a survey of the beautiful court, she chose a table at the far edge that overlooked an expanse of green grass.

After they were seated, the hostess placed menus in front of them and promised a waiter would be right with them.

Once the woman had walked away, Tallulah sat back in her seat and stared around her in wonder. "I'm in shock."

Her remark clearly amused him.

"Why? This is a nice place, but it's not overly ritzy."

She shook her head. "I'm shocked because it's such a romantic setting. How did you come about eating here? Or maybe I shouldn't ask," she added with a clever grin.

The faint grin on his face deepened. "I wasn't here with a woman, if that's what you're thinking. I was here for a wedding. One of the barn workers married a woman from Cave Creek, and the ceremony was held here on the patio with dinner being served afterward."

"Hmm. So they have weddings at this place," she said thoughtfully. "I'm not surprised. I feel like we've entered a tropical fairyland. But you've surprised me—again. I can't imagine you attending a wedding."

He shrugged. "Daniel is a nice guy, and he's always ready to help me with whatever is going on at the barn. I made the effort for him."

He was loyal to his friends, Tallulah thought. And she didn't have to wonder if he'd been a loyal husband. Even after several years of widowhood, he was still devoted to the memory of his wife. But she didn't want to think about that tonight. No, she wanted to believe that it was only the two of them sitting here together in this slice of desert paradise.

Hours later, as Jim parked the truck in front of his house, Tallulah said, "The dinner was scrumptious and the trip was wonderful. Maybe we can do it again in the not-too-distant future. Only the next time, I'll drive us and pay for the meal."

"Oh no. Not on your life." He shut off the engine and turned to her. "That's my responsibility."

Amused, she shook her head. "Why? If it's my idea to make a return trip, then I should foot the bill."

"Not with me," he said, then reached over and squeezed her hand. "It's a man thing, Tallulah. No, let me change that to—it's more of a cowboy thing."

She leveled a suggestive smile at him. "Is it a cowboy thing to invite me in for coffee? I know it's getting late, but I'm not ready for our evening to end. Are you?"

If Jim were honest with himself, he was never ready for his time with Tallulah to end. But for some reason he couldn't say those telling words to her. He was still finding it hard to say anything that might lead her to believe he was getting serious about the two of them being together. Deep down he knew he wasn't being fair to her or himself. But for so long now, he'd closed himself off to showing affection, to caring and loving. He was just now learning how to let himself feel again. He wasn't yet capable of expressing those feelings to her in words.

Will you ever be capable, Jim? Or do you plan on hiding behind a wall of disappointment and grief for the rest of your life. If you don't find some backbone soon, you're going to become a loser in the love department.

Love, hell! Jim cursed at the taunting voice in

his head. He didn't want love. He only wanted a little happiness without all the strings and worries of a passionate romance.

He said, "I wasn't about to let you get away this early, Tallulah."

She laughed softly, and the sound caused a funny little curl in the pit of his stomach.

"And I wasn't about to leave," she said.

He helped her out of the truck, and the two of them entered the house. Jim had left a night-light burning in the living room, and the dim glow was enough to illuminate a section of the couch and nearby armchair.

With Tallulah at his side, he said, "I'll turn on a lamp so we can see to get to the kitchen."

Her hand suddenly wrapped around his forearm, and he looked at her in question.

"I don't really need coffee right now," she said. "Do you?"

Her brown eyes were glittering, and there was no mistaking the desire he heard in her voice. The sound echoed the longing that had been growing in him all evening.

Turning toward her, he slipped his arms around her waist and gathered her close to him.

"No. I don't need anything. Except you," he whispered.

"Oh, Jim."

The two words were all she said before she raised on tiptoes and angled her lips up to his.

He didn't waste the invitation to kiss her. Capturing her lips beneath his, he tugged her closer, until the front of her body was crushed against the length of his. Instantly, her arms slipped around his neck and her mouth opened to his.

The hungry kiss immediately turned fiery, causing their lips to clamp together and their tongues to engage in a sensual give and take. Hot desire shot straight to his brain, then ricocheted downward until it settled like a bucket of burning coals in his loins.

The honeyed taste of her lips was as familiar to him as if he'd kissed her a thousand times, while smoothing his hands over the soft curves of her body was like finding a pleasure he'd hidden away and had finally rediscovered.

When the need for oxygen finally forced his mouth to ease away from hers, he mouthed in a husky voice against her hair. "Tallulah, you feel so good in my arms. You taste better than anything I've ever tasted in my life."

"You can't know how much I want you, Jim. How much I need for you to hold me. Love me," she whispered urgently.

Her hands met at the front of his shirt and began to fumble with the snaps. Jim stood stock-still until the garment had parted and her hands were lying flat against his bare chest. After that, he claimed her mouth once again and this time the kiss he placed upon her lips was so hungry and all-consuming that for long moments he forgot where he was, or even who he was. All he knew was that he wanted Tallulah more than he wanted his next breath.

When the sound of her weak moan finally registered in his foggy brain, he lifted his head and gazed down at her swollen lips and the tumble of dark hair that had dipped over her closed eyes. Her sexy image very nearly choked him with wanton desire.

"I want you, too, Tallulah. So much. Too much." Bringing his hands up to her shoulders, he somehow found the willpower to put some space between them. "But you're asking me to take a leap into something...I'm not sure I'm ready for."

Her expression was incredulous as she stood staring at him. "Are you serious? Really? Because it sure as heck felt like you were ready."

He mouthed a curse under his breath even as his body was screaming for him to pull her back into his arms.

"Yeah, my body is more than ready," he muttered. "But not my brain."

She opened her mouth, and Jim expected her to snap a sharp retort at him. Instead, she turned and moved to a spot in the room where the glow of the night-light ended and darkness began.

Standing with her back to him, she said, "Okay, Jim. Okay. I give up. Your head is clearly somewhere else. It's also obvious that your head is going to stay…in the past. I've—"

"Tallulah, you—"

She interrupted before he could go on. "No, Jim! Let me finish. Because I can see now that I'm the one who's made a mistake. I've been carrying around hopes that you would change. That you'd want us to be together. Really together. I kept thinking time was all you needed to accept the idea of us becoming intimate. But time is just a stupid excuse I've been using to keep my hopes alive. You've had years of time to get over your late wife, but they've done little to fix you. It might be a thrill for you to lead me on and then let me down, but it's downright hell for me."

Anger and disbelief shot through him. "A thrill! Do I look happy?"

Laughing shrilly, she turned to stare at him. "Happy? That's hilarious! You don't want to be happy or anything close to it. You'd rather cling to your grief like a safety blanket."

Blood was boiling in his head, but to his dismay it was still simmering in his loins and making him ache for a release that only she could give him.

Dear Lord, was he losing his grip on his mind, or body, or both?

"That's a horrible thing to say!"

"No more horrible than the way you're treating me!" she shot back at him. "And frankly, I don't intend to take any more."

He watched in shocked wonder as she started toward the door. "What are you doing? Running out?"

Pausing at the opening of the entryway, she looked at him and he could see her expression was taut with anger and frustration. He'd never seen her like this, and the repercussion from the shock was shaking thick scales from his eyes.

"No. I'm coming to my senses, Jim. When or if you ever decide you want to be a real partner to me, you know where I'll be."

"Sex! Is that all you want from me?"

Her lips were compressed to a straight line as she marched over and stood in front of him.

"Never in my life have I wanted to slap anyone— until this very moment!" she exclaimed, seething with anger. "You think sex is what I want from you? Sorry, Jim, but I want far more than sex!"

She turned and walked rapidly toward the door, and as Jim watched her go, he realized there would be no second chances with her. If he allowed her to drive away, everything between them would be finished.

The desolate thought sent him trotting after her, and he managed to catch up to her just as she was about to open the door.

With a hand on her shoulder, he turned her around and straight into his arms.

"What—"

"Don't leave, Tallulah."

Her eyes crackled with anger as her gaze raced over his face. "I'm tired of talking, Jim!"

"So am I," he fired back at her. "Tired of talking. And thinking!"

Before she could guess his intentions, he gathered her into the circle of his arms and covered her lips with a kiss that exposed all the frustration and hunger that was tying his insides into painful knots.

With a groan of surrender, her mouth opened and met his kiss with a driving force that matched his own.

He kissed her until they were both winded and, as they both drew in ragged gulps of air, Jim was shocked to discover his legs had turned spongy and his heart had jumped into such a rapid pace he was amazed that it hadn't stopped beating entirely.

"I can't bear this, Jim," she whispered in an anguished voice. "I don't want us to end. But these mixed signals you're giving me are too much—too confusing for me to deal with."

With his hands cupping the sides of her face,

he tilted her head back in order to look directly into her eyes.

"I don't want to confuse you, Tallulah," he said, his voice rough with desire. "I want you to know exactly what I want—and need."

Doubt flickered in her eyes, and then her lips began to tremble. "Are you serious? Because if you're not, then I want you to let me go."

Let her go? How could he do that when looking at the future without her was like staring into a dark, bottomless pit.

"Let me show you how serious."

Ignoring her skeptical expression, he took her by the hand and led her through the living room, then down a shadowy hallway and through an open door on the left.

As they entered his bedroom, he said, "Before I turn a light on, you should probably close your eyes, Tallulah. The bed isn't made and over in the corner there's a pile of dirty clothes on the floor."

Turning, she wrapped her arms around his waist and snuggled the front of her body next to his. "Who needs a light? Or a tidy bedroom? All I want is for us to make love—for you to be thinking about me and nothing else."

"These evenings we've spent together I've been fighting like hell against this. And now I'm thinking I must have been out of my mind. How did I think I was going to resist you? Or this?"

"Up until a few minutes ago you were doing a fairly good job of it," she said pointedly.

He drew her lips a breath away from his. "Thank you, Tallulah. For waking me up—and forcing me to see what a fool I've been."

"Maybe we've both been fools. But that's all over," she said softly.

He kissed her cheeks and chin and finally her lips before he slipped an arm around the back of her waist and guided her through the shadows until they reached the side of the double bed.

"Yes." His hands reached for the zipper on the back of her dress and gently pulled it downward. "That's all over. And the two of us are just beginning."

And as her dress fell to the floor and his hands spanned her slender waist, he was stunned at just how much he meant those words.

Chapter Nine

Tallulah's entire body quivered with need as Jim tossed her lacey undergarments atop her dress on the floor and his hands began a slow seductive search of her breasts, the flare of her hips, then across the lower part of her belly. At the same time his fingers were creating magic upon her skin, he was kissing a heated trail down the side of her neck, across her collarbone and farther down to where her budded nipples were waiting impatiently for the touch of his lips.

When it finally came, she cried out with pleasure and arched her body toward his. His tongue lathed each nipple for long, long moments before he eventually moved his attention downward to the shallow indentation of her naval. As he nipped the soft skin of her belly, she felt desire building in the lower part of her body, while every sensible thought flew out of her head.

"Do you realize how good you're making me feel? How alive I am now that you're touching me like this?" Her voice was so thick with desire, she barely recognized it. But then, she hardly recognized herself. Not like this. With Jim touching her, loving her as though he really meant it, as though he wanted her more than anything in his life.

He brought his mouth back up to hers. "I'm feeling the same way," he said against her lips. "And I'm thinking I've wasted so much time. Precious time that I could've had you in my arms—my bed."

With his hands on each side of her waist, he started to lift her up and onto the bed, but the pressure on his hand caused him to stop and wince with pain.

"Damn," he said. "I can't even lift you onto the bed."

She reached for his bandaged hand and drew it to her lips. After gently kissing the injured palm, she said, "I don't care about that. In fact, since you're having to do things with one hand you need to let me help you get out of your clothes."

His lips twisted to a wry slant. "I'm not that helpless."

She purposely made her chuckle a sound of seduction. "Have you stopped to think I might *want* to undress you?"

"If that's the case," he said huskily, "I wouldn't dare try to stop you."

"I like the sound of that."

She quickly finished unsnapping his shirt and then pushed it off his shoulders. While his lips nibbled at her neck, she wanted to give her hands a chance to explore his muscled chest, but she was in too big of a hurry to get him undressed and experience the length of his naked body against hers.

In her haste, her fingers fumbled with his belt and the zipper of his jeans. And the fact that he was placing distracting little kisses along the base of her throat made the task even more of a challenge. But she finally managed to unfasten both and push the denim down his hips.

"Um, Jim, I can't get your jeans off with your boots still on."

Lifting his head, he grinned at her. "I guess you can tell I'm not used to having a woman undress me."

Slanting him a provocative smile, she said, "I'm not exactly experienced in undressing cowboys, either."

He sat down on the edge of the bed and allowed Tallulah to remove his dark brown boots and socks. After she'd placed the footwear out of the way, she pulled the denim down over his feet and tossed the pair of jeans in the direction of her dress.

When she finally reached for the waistband of

his briefs, he wrapped a hand around her wrist to prevent her from making him completely nude.

"We'll do that later," he whispered, then gestured behind him at the tumbled bedclothes. "Maybe we should do something about those messy covers first."

Smiling, she eased down beside him on the bed. "I don't care about the bedcovers. All I care about is having you next to me."

He drew the both of them down against the mattress until they were lying face-to-face and his forehead was resting against hers.

His breath warmed her cheeks as he gently brushed his lips across hers, and the tantalizing touch caused her to groan with need.

Curling her arm around his waist, she pulled the front of her body closer to his and reveled in the incredible sensation of having her breasts pressed against the hard muscles of his chest, to feel his legs entwined with hers. His skin was hot, and the heat seeped deep into her flesh.

She couldn't begin to guess how long they kissed, she only knew his mouth was making magic on hers, while his hands were skimming over every inch of her body until she was certain if he didn't stop she would soon burst into flames.

He must have felt her frustration because he suddenly lifted his head and looked down at her. With his gaze locked on hers, his hand slipped between the juncture of her thighs, where, ever so gently, his fingers brushed the folds of her womanhood. The touch instinctively caused her knees to part and give him free access to touch that intimate part of her.

Her voice was strangled with desire when she finally managed to speak, "Oh, Jim—if you keep that up you're going to make me fly away."

He fingers continued to tease her. "Mmm. That's what I want you to do."

He lowered his mouth to hers, and as their mouths locked together in another heated kiss, his finger slipped inside to stroke the part of her that was desperately aching to connect with his body.

The contact was so incredible, so fiercely wonderful she could hardly bear the pleasure. Mindlessly, she released a string of guttural moans and arched her hips eagerly upward. The movement drew his finger even deeper into her, and in the span of a few seconds she began to twist and writhe against his hand.

Tearing his mouth from hers, he whispered near her ear. "Let yourself fly, sweetheart. I promise you'll land right back here in my arms."

His words were enough to snap the last of her control and suddenly she was leaping into an inky sky filled with a million blazing stars. Her mind momentarily went blank, and then slowly she became aware of Jim's arms holding her close, absorbing the tremors of her release.

She was attempting to gather her breath when she felt him ease away from her and leave the bed. Eventually, she managed to open her eyes to see him standing in front of the nightstand, rifling through the contents of the top drawer.

Rising up on one elbow, she started to ask him what he was doing, but thankfully, before the thoughtless question could pass her lips, it dawned on her that he was searching for a condom.

Tallulah could've told him not to bother. After her divorce, she'd continued to take oral birth control for reasons other than being intimate with a man. But she quickly decided to keep the information to herself. She wanted him to feel safe. And the extra protection would cut the chance of an unexpected pregnancy. A situation that would hardly foster their budding relationship.

Once he had himself fitted with the condom, he turned back to the bed, and Tallulah didn't waste any time patting the empty space at her side.

Her invitation put a half grin on his lips. "What's wrong? Afraid I'm going to squash you?"

She gave him a clever smile. "I'm hardly that fragile. But I doubt you can hold your weight up with one hand. Well, maybe you could, but it wouldn't be easy. I know a better way to solve the problem."

"You do?"

She pulled him down beside her and with her hands on both shoulders, pushed until she had him lying flat against the mattress.

"Yes, I do," she murmured. "And I want to make this special for you."

He growled with hungry anticipation, and before she could get her body draped completely over his, he curved a hand around the back of her neck and drew her mouth down to his.

"It already is special," he said as he captured her lips in another heated kiss.

Desire scorched the lower half of her body, and without breaking the contact of their lips, she straddled his hips and lowered herself onto his hardened shaft.

The contact was so intense that stars sparked behind her closed eyelids, and somewhere beyond the wild roaring in her ears, she heard his throaty groan.

Lifting her head, she looked down at him, and as their gazes met, she felt certain only the two of them were in his bed and his mind.

"Tallulah. Sweet Tallulah."

With her hands anchored on his broad shoulders, she began to move her hips slowly and temptingly against him. But all too quickly, hot need forced her to quicken the tempo of her thrusts. Jim matched her rhythm and soon they were bound together in a fierce battle to see which one of them could give and receive the most.

The room began to spin around her, and as the intensity of their union grew, Tallulah lost all awareness of her surroundings. All she knew was that she was climbing a stairway and each step was taking her closer to paradise.

Beneath her, the sharp, quick intakes of his breaths matched her own, and she wondered if, like her, he was reaching the point of exhaustion.

"I can't...go on, Jim! I—"

Her breathless plea came to an abrupt halt as his hands fastened over her buttocks and clamped her so tightly against him that it was impossible to move her hips. All she could do was hang on to his shoulders and wait for him to give her some sort of relief.

"Yes! Oh yes...you can go on. We...both...can."

The garbled words barely passed his lips when Tallulah felt herself slipping into a starlit abyss.

The frantic fall had her fingers clenching his flesh, and then as his strong arms fastened tightly around her, she realized she wasn't falling at all. The two of them were drifting together in a velvety space. Slowly, back and forth, they rocked in sweet oblivion, until her sweat-drenched body collapsed on top of him.

A few moments passed before Tallulah found enough energy to roll her weight off the top of him. Yet even then, she didn't want to break the contact of their bodies.

Snuggling up to his side, she pillowed her cheek upon his shoulder and rested a hand on his chest. Beneath her palm, she could feel his heart pounding madly, while his chest rose and fell as his lungs labored to replenish his body with oxygen.

"Are you okay?" she asked gently.

Grunting, he brought his hand against her hair. "I'm supposed to be asking you that question. Not the other way around."

She tilted her head until her chin was resting upon his collarbone and her eyes were looking directly into his.

"I'm incredibly wonderful," she told him.

His features softened. "Incredibly wonderful," he repeated. "Yes. I feel that way, too."

She touched fingertips to his cheek. "You do? Really?"

He wound a strand of her hair around his forefinger. "You have to ask me that after what just happened between us?"

A lopsided grin twisted her lips. "Well, you weren't exactly wanting me in your bedroom."

Groaning with misgivings, his hands slipped to the small of her back and drew her closer to him. "What I was saying earlier tonight didn't exactly match what I was feeling."

Her heart was full of raw emotions as she

reached up and pushed a hank of tawny hair from his forehead. "I don't want you to have regrets."

"No regrets. Now if I had been stupid enough to let you walk out the door, then I would've been loaded with regrets."

Tears suddenly burned the backs of her eyes and she was forced to blink several times and swallow before she was able to speak.

"You know what? This is the first time in my life that I'm glad I had a blowout."

A quizzical look came over his face, and then he laughed outright.

"You know what, Tallulah? I'm glad you had a blowout, too."

There was freedom and joy in his voice that she'd not heard in him until tonight, and the sound infused her heart with hope.

If he could allow himself to be truly happy again, then surely he could let himself love once more.

The following Tuesday, Jim's visit at the doctor's office resulted in getting the stitches removed from his hand and the cumbersome bandage reduced to a wide Band-Aid across his palm.

Before he'd started the drive back to Three Rivers, Jim had texted Tallulah to give her the good news, and she'd promptly sent him an emoji in the shape of a heart.

The image had made him smile. It had also made him realize just how much his life had changed since he'd met her on the road nearly three weeks ago. At that time if someone had told him he'd be making love to a beautiful brunette, he would've declared the person crazy. Now he could think of little else.

The night he and Tallulah had returned from the trip to Cave Creek and he'd ended up taking her to bed had shaken him in a way that still had him marveling. He'd been so afraid to give in to her. Yet once he'd had her in his arms it was like everything right and good had fallen into place.

Since then, she'd been coming over every night to be with him, and the more they were together, the more he wanted her. Jim realized she was monopolizing his thoughts and even a part of his heart, but he didn't care. Holt had told him more than once that a guy deserved a second chance at the things that mattered most in his life. And Jim was beginning to recognize that Tallulah was his second chance at happiness. He couldn't squander it.

Upon his return from town, Jim entered the horse barn and was heading to Holt's office to give his boss an update on the doctor's visit when Colt called to him.

"Hey, Jim, how's the hand?"

Pausing, Jim turned to see his friend and co-worker walking rapidly toward him.

He held up his hand to let Colt see the bandage had been replaced with a Band-Aid. "Great. Look at this. I feel like I've been let out of jail. The stitches are out, and the gash is almost healed."

"Good," Colt told him. "I hope I never see you trying to trim the buckskin's feet again. He's wicked. Everyone on the ranch seems to know it, except you."

Jim shrugged. "What can I say, Colt. I like a challenge, and I expect I'll take another stab at doing Buck's feet again real soon."

Shaking his head, Colt said, "Man, you have to be the bravest guy I've ever known, or the stupidest."

"That's what I say every time you get on Daisy Mae," Jim told him.

The young filly had been a wild thing when Colt had first started breaking her to the saddle. That had been back in December. Since then, she'd quit bucking, but Daisy still played dirty at times.

Colt laughed. "Well, a guy has to test his courage from time to time."

Jim glanced down the wide alleyway of the barn, then over his shoulder toward Holt's office. "Where is everyone? It's quiet as a tomb in here."

"Holt sent most of the men out to round up the remuda in the south pasture. The rest of the barn workers are hauling manure out to the compost pile, and Luke is out in the training arena. In fact, he's waiting on me to bring him a hackamore from the tack room. I'd better get going."

"Oh. Well, I was on my way to give Holt a report on my hand," Jim told him. "Now he can quit worrying about me busting my stitches. As soon as I see him, I'll be out to help you guys."

Frowning, Colt shook his head. "Uh…Holt isn't here. While you were gone to town, he was called away. Something about Isabelle not feeling well. I think he was going to take her to see her obstetrician."

Rocked by the news, Jim stared at his friend. "Isabelle is sick?"

Colt shrugged. "I'm not sure. Luke is the person Holt spoke with before he left the ranch. And Luke implied to me that the call had something to do with the baby."

Isabelle was headed into the sixth month of a third pregnancy. Maybe the stress of carrying another baby so soon after giving birth to Axel and running her horse ranch was all too much for the woman, he thought.

"That's…uh…not good," Jim said, while trying not to let his mind travel back to Lyndsey and his own lost baby.

"No. But Luke and I are hoping it's nothing serious. I figure Holt will let us know something as soon as he can."

"Yeah. Let's hope so," Jim told him.

* * *

Later that evening Tallulah had the children gathered in the upstairs playroom when Katherine walked through the door.

As soon as the twins spotted their mother, they jumped up from the game they were playing on the floor and raced over to greet her. She laughingly hugged them to her side.

"Wow. You two must have really missed me while I was at work!" she said to the twins, then winked at Tallulah as she joined them.

"We did miss you, Mommy!" Abagail exclaimed.

"A whole lot!" Andrew seconded his sister.

Katherine said, "Well, I have news for you two. Mommy has tomorrow off. School is letting out for a teachers' conference. So that means you children don't have to go to school. And I was thinking we might all go to town and visit the park. That is if Nanny Tally is willing to go and help with the five of you."

"Oh boy!" Andrew shouted. "We wanta go."

Abagail looked beseechingly up at Tallulah. "Do you wanta go, too, Nanny Tally?"

"Of course," Tallulah assured the girl. "I wouldn't want to miss a trip to the park."

Abagail clapped her hands while Andrew jumped up and down. "It'll be fun," he said. "Can we take sandwiches and soda?"

"No, Andy," Abagail said in a haughty tone as she turned her nose up to the air. "You don't take soda on a picnic. You take lemonade."

As soon as Abagail attempted to correct her brother, the argument was on.

Laughing, Katherine shooed them over to where Evelyn and Billy and little Madison were busy building a wall of brightly colored plastic blocks.

"Stop arguing and go tell your cousins about the park," she said, then, with a hopeless shake of her head, smiled at Tallulah. "I really think you're a saint. How do you deal with all five of them together at one time?"

"It's easy. They mostly keep me laughing," she said, then asked, "Were you serious about the trip to the park?"

"Yes. Actually, I was. Why? Had you rather not deal with taking the whole group? It might be easier on you if we left Maddie here with her mother. But I'd hate for the little girl to miss out on the fun, too."

"Oh no. I think it's great. And I wouldn't want to go without Maddie. I just thought…well, Maureen just told Jazelle and I a few minutes ago that the doctor admitted Isabelle into the hospital."

The smile fell from Katherine's face as her hand came to rest on her pregnant belly. "Yes. Unfortunately, she's having some problems. From what I've been told, the doctor is taking precautionary measures to make sure that she and the baby remain healthy. She'll be getting some medication, and she has to keep quiet and rested. Which means very limited visitors for her—only Holt and her mother. So as far as Isabelle is concerned, there's really nothing we can do, but wait and pray."

Tallulah nodded. "I assure you that I'll be praying for her and the baby. And Kat, I'd be happy to care for Carter and Axel if Holt needs help with them. Adding two more children to the mix won't be a problem."

"That's generous of you to offer, Tallulah, but for right now I believe Isabelle's mother, Gabby, has the boys with her. If she ends up needing your help, I'll let you know."

"Yes. Please do."

After speaking with Katherine and driving over to Jim's house, she was feeling far more optimistic about Isabelle. Still, it was a relief when he opened the door and she could wrap her arms around him.

Pressing her cheek to the middle of his chest, she hugged him tight. "Mmm. It feels so good to have your arms around me. It's been a bit of a trying day. And being with you makes it all better."

He planted a kiss on the top of her head. "Having trouble with the kids today?"

She eased out of his arms, and as the two of them walked into the living room, she said, "No. I found plenty of things to keep the children occupied, and there wasn't much fussing going on between them. To be honest, the news about Isabelle has knocked me a bit off-kilter. Have you heard she's in the hospital?"

He stopped in his tracks and looked at her. "No! Colt told me that Holt had taken her to the doctor. Nothing about the hospital. When did this happen?"

The alarm she saw on his face wasn't the normal concern shown for a friend; he looked stricken. His reaction puzzled Tallulah. But then he'd worked for the Hollisters for years, she thought. No doubt he was close friends to all of them, including Isabelle.

"Late this afternoon. It's a precautionary move by the doctor. But I can't help but feel anxious for her. I've not had a chance to be around Isabelle that much. But the few times I've been in her presence, I was a bit in awe. She's so beautiful and nice. And everyone can see that she and Holt are madly in love with each other, and they adore their two little boys."

"Yes. The two of them are solid."

Solid? That was hardly the way Tallulah would describe the loving couple. "Well, I always looked at them like a family made in heaven, you know? But I suppose even perfect families encounter problems from time to time."

He grimaced. "No family is perfect, Tallulah. Not even Holt's or Blake's or Vivian's or any of the Hollisters."

Confused by his sardonic attitude, she glanced at him. "What's with all the pessimism? When I said perfect, I didn't mean it literally. I only meant that they're happy and together and they love one another. If a person has those things, then yes, I'd say that's the closest thing to perfection."

He drew in a deep breath, then blew it out. "Sorry, Tallulah. I didn't mean to sound so cynical. It's just that I'm concerned for the both of them. Holt is like a brother to me. During all these years I've been working on the ranch, he's had my back. Whenever I get down, he's always been there to lift me up and keep me going. Now his wife and child are in danger, and I feel damned helpless because there's nothing I can do for him."

Now that she understood where his dark mind-set was coming from, she was struck with the need to comfort him.

Wrapping an arm around his waist, she hugged him to her side. "Don't worry, Jim. Holt will see that Isabelle has the best of care. And I truly believe everything will turn out good. And so should you."

His blue eyes were solemn as they met hers, but after a moment a faint smile touched the corners of his lips. "Okay. I'll do my best to be optimistic."

"I'm happy to hear it," she said in the cheeriest voice she could muster. "And now, since I didn't bring supper with me, what do you say we go find something in your fridge to eat? I'm game for the leftover spaghetti from last night if you are."

"Sure." He held up his palm to show her the simple Band-Aid. "Now that I'm rid of that darned bandage, I'll show you I'm good help in the kitchen. I can even wash dishes—when I get the urge."

She chuckled knowingly. "And how often is that?"

His grin was sheepish, and Tallulah was relieved to see his spirits had lifted.

"Oh, maybe two or three times a week. Or when I run out of dishes."

Hooking her arm through his, she urged him toward the kitchen. "Come on. I've got to see this."

Throughout the meal, Jim tried his best to smile and make sensible conversation with Tallulah, but the effort was draining every ounce of energy he had. Which wasn't much given the busy day he'd put in at the horse barn.

Damn it, why couldn't he forget the past and simply look at the present and the future? Why had he allowed Isabelle's situation with the baby trigger all those dark, tragic memories he'd tried to hide away? He understood his morose reaction was unhealthy. He even knew that in many ways he was being a coward for not being able to take Tallulah aside and explain everything that had happened to him nine years ago. He'd managed to talk to her about Lyndsey's death. Why hadn't he gone a step further and told her about his son and how he'd lost the baby after six short days?

Because it was too painful, he grimly answered himself. Because he didn't want Tallulah to know that he was too emotionally weak to face up to the loss of Cody. He couldn't let her know how the mere thought of trying to have another child filled him with icy fear. No, she might understand up to a point, he thought. But in the end, she wouldn't want an emotionally crippled man in her life. And she especially wouldn't want one for a husband.

"Jim? Are you okay?"

Tallulah's voice managed to penetrate his deep thoughts, and he looked over to see she was frowning at him.

"Uh…yeah. I'm fine. Sorry. I was thinking about…something at work."

Her expression dubious, she said, "I was asking if you'd like something for dessert. I think there are a few pastries left from those I brought over yesterday."

"I've had plenty. You go ahead and have one."

She rose from her chair and carried her plate over to the sink. "I think I've had plenty, too."

Sometime during the meal, the cheery note in her voice had disappeared, and Jim wondered if she'd been reading his thoughts. He needed her to be smiling even if he couldn't.

Picking up his dirty plate and utensils, he joined her at the cabinet and placed them next to the sink she'd filled with warm, sudsy water.

"I'm doing the dishes tonight," he said. "Remember?"

Smiling faintly, she picked up his hand and closely examined the tan-colored strip of adhesive plastered to his palm. "I know your hand is all better. But you shouldn't get it wet. I can handle kitchen duties—until you're completely healed."

Completely healed. A few days of time had done wonders to heal his hand, he thought, but years of time hadn't completely healed his heart. Yet he had to hope and believe that loving Tallulah was going to change him.

Love! What the hell was he thinking? He didn't love Tallulah. He liked her and wanted her. He even cared about her. But love was something different. He wasn't capable of feeling that much. He didn't want to feel that much.

Did he?

He lifted his hands, and as he cradled both sides of her face, an odd crushing pressure suddenly hit the middle of his chest. He didn't know where the pain had come from or why it had hit him at this very moment. But he figured Tallulah was the only remedy that would make it go away.

"Let's forget get about the dishes," he whispered.

Her eyelids drooped and her mouth softened. "You have something better in mind to do?"

His hands slipped to her back and he trailed his fingers across the smooth warm skin. "I can think of plenty," he said huskily. "Starting with this."

He fastened his lips over hers, and she was quick to respond to his kiss. And just as Jim had expected, the weird little pain beneath his breastbone disappeared as quickly as it came.

Two hours later, Tallulah was curled against Jim in his warm bed, and her leg was casually draped across his thighs. Through half-closed eyes, she watched the steady rise and fall of his chest and wondered what was occupying his thoughts. And more importantly what was going on inside his heart.

This past week, she'd been coming here every evening after her nanny duties were finished, and she'd been staying until twelve or one o'clock in the morning. With each passing night, Tallulah had felt the two of them growing closer, and every time Jim had made love to her, she'd felt him giving more and more of himself to her. And throughout these past days, she couldn't remember a time she'd felt happier or more hopeful about her future.

Only minutes ago, they'd finished making love again, and just as the times before, he'd taken her on a magical trip. Yet tonight she'd felt an urgency in him that she'd never felt before. And the fact that he'd not bothered to say a word to her since they'd been lying quietly in the darkness weighed heavily on her heart.

Yes, he was worried about Holt. She could see that. But did worry about his friend give him a reason to push her completely out of his thoughts?

"Jim, are you okay?"

His brows pulled together as he turned his head toward hers. "Why do you keep asking if I'm okay?"

The annoyance in his voice cut her deep. "Did you ever stop to think I'm asking because I'm concerned about you?"

"Why? Do I look sick? I just had a doctor's visit this morning. He pronounced me fit."

"Yes, your hand is nearly well. But I don't expect he examined your head."

She rolled away from him and sat up on the side of the bed.

"What is that supposed to mean?" he asked.

She breathed deeply in an attempt to stem her rising temper. "Nothing. I'm sorry I said it. I can see that—" She glanced over her shoulder to see he was sitting cross-legged in the middle of the bed, and her heart winced at the sight of his troubled face. "You have...other things on your mind."

"How do you know what's on my mind? I might be thinking about you."

She closed her eyes and swallowed at the lump

of emotion that seemed to be growing with each passing second.

"You've not had much to say this whole evening."

He mouthed a curse word. "Am I supposed to be a chatterbox all the time?"

Standing, she reached for her undergarments. While she put on her bra and panties, she said, "No. You can be as quiet as a little mouse if you want. I'm going home."

"Home. It's still early!" he exclaimed.

Surprised that he even cared, she looked at him. "Yes. But you've had a long day. And I need to be rested for tomorrow. Kat has the day off, and she wants the two of us to take the kids to the park in town."

A quizzical frown wrinkled his brow. "To the park! Are you serious?"

"Well, yes. What's wrong with treating the children? It's good for them to do and see different things."

"That's true," he replied. "But isn't that being a bit insensitive? Going to the park with Isabelle in the hospital?"

Turning back toward the bed, she struggled to keep from shouting at him. "Before you start labeling us as uncaring, you need to know a few facts. Isabelle is in the hospital for complete quiet and rest. Her visitors are limited to Holt and her mother, Gabby. No one else is allowed in. I suppose Kat and I and the children could drive to the hospital and sit outside in the parking lot all day, but I doubt that would do Isabelle much good. What do you think?"

Lifting his face toward the ceiling, he raked both hands roughly through his hair. "I think I sound like a jerk and have been acting even worse. I'm sorry, Tallulah. Truly."

The remorseful tone in his voice was enough to chase away her frustration and with a groan of surrender, she eased down on the side of the bed and placed a hand on his forearm.

"I believe you," she said gently.

He scooted to the edge of the bed and gathered her into the circle of his arms. "Then you'll stay a little longer? At least until midnight," he added with a rueful grin.

She couldn't resist him. Not when his strong arms were filling her with warmth and his blue eyes were making all sorts of delicious promises.

Slipping her arms around his neck, she rested her cheek against his. "Aren't you taking a chance?" she whispered close to his ear. "Come midnight I might turn into a real shrew."

"I'll take that chance," he murmured. His fingers reached to the middle of her back to unhook her bra, and once the lacy garment fell away, he pushed her back down on the mattress.

"You really didn't have to talk me into staying," she said impishly. "I couldn't have left even if I'd wanted to. Georgette has made her bed on my jeans. And I didn't have the heart to disturb her."

He brought his lips around to hers. "Remind me to give that cat some extra treats."

"Mmm. If you don't mind, I'll take my treats right here and now."

She pressed herself closer to his hard body, and as his kiss turned into a hungry search, her only thought was being in his arms and believing the two of them would always be together.

But what's going to happen if the ghost of his wife walks into this room, Tallulah? Can you build a happy life with a man who has another woman on his mind?

As Jim continued to kiss her, the mocking question tried to stay in Tallulah's head. But soon his heated lovemaking pushed it away, and all that was left in her thoughts was the hope that she was strong enough to fight off any ghost who tried to tear them apart.

Chapter Ten

Jim was bent over a mare's hind hoof, pushing an iron rasp over its edge, when from the corner of his right eye he spotted a pair of boots coming to a halt a few steps in front of him. He recognized the scuffed and scarred roughout boots as belonging to Colt.

"I've come to the conclusion that Holt is wasting his money on hiring a professional farrier to come out to the ranch twice a month. He doesn't need one. Not with you around."

Not bothering to look up, Jim responded with a grunt. "I'm not a professional. I've just done this job for so long that everyone thinks I am."

Satisfied that the mare's hoof was shaped correctly, he lowered her foot to the ground and gave her hip an affectionate pat.

Looking over at Colt, he asked, "Need another one saddled? Or are you calling it quits for today?"

Colt pushed back the cuff of his shirt and glanced at his watch. "Too early to quit. There's still a bit of daylight left. But I can take care of the saddling. I came over here to ask a favor of you. I don't like doing it, but I'm in a tight spot right now."

"What kind of favor?" Jim was instantly suspicious. Colt wasn't one to ask for favors and when he did, it usually involved doing something dangerous. "You must want me to ride snubbed up to you. On that sorrel you're trying to break."

Grinning, Colt said, "Jim, you're the most mistrustful guy I know. I promise I'm not trying to get your neck broken. What I really need is for you to do barn duty tonight. Riggs had to leave the ranch a few minutes ago to deal with a personal matter. He can't be back until morning. And Farley is sick with some kind of stomach bug. I've sent him to the bunkhouse. There's no one else I'd trust but you. Or myself. But I've promised Sophia I'd take her to the Broken Spur tonight for supper."

"The Spur?"

Jim's look of disbelief had Colt laughing. "Yeah, go figure. She loves the place. And seeing the woman has promised to marry me, I'm trying to keep her happy."

There was no doubt that Colt was keeping his

fiancée happy. The horseman wasn't afraid to show her how much he loved her. Nor was he shying away from making a future with her. Unlike Jim, who'd been fighting tooth and nail to keep his emotions bottled tightly inside him.

But that was the safe way, Jim thought. The only way he knew to keep from being hurt.

"No problem. I can do barn duty."

"Thanks. I feel bad about asking. You work your butt off around here. You don't need to be on the job for twenty-four hours."

Shaking his head, Jim said, "I figure things will be quiet. I'll catch some sleep."

He just wouldn't be holding Tallulah's soft warm body. Which might be for the best, Jim thought ruefully. A week had passed since that night she'd threatened to go home early and, since then, God only knew how hard Jim had tried to be better company for her. But the more he tried to be an attentive partner, the more he feared he was swimming into deeper and deeper water.

"Thanks, Jim. You can take off tomorrow if you want."

Jim's scoffing laugh told Colt what he could do with that idea. "I'm not taking any damned day off!" he muttered and then, because he couldn't help himself, he asked, "Uh…have you heard anything from Holt today? I thought I saw his truck here earlier, but I didn't find him in his office."

"He was here for a few minutes, but Luke and I ran him off. With Isabelle still in the hospital, he has to keep everything at Blue Stallion Ranch going. He said the hands are doing a good job. But there are still plenty of things he has to attend to himself."

"What about Isabelle? What does he say about her condition?"

Colt shrugged. "Not much change. Everything is stable. But the doctor doesn't feel confident about letting her out of bed or the hospital. Holt said the OB has changed her medication and everyone is hoping it's going to fix the problem."

Jim didn't bother to hide his cynicism. "Hoping, yeah. Everyone is hoping. But is that going to fix anything?"

Frowning at him, Colt said, "It's a heck of a lot better than thinking the worst."

The barn manager didn't give Jim time to make a reply. Which hardly mattered. He couldn't contradict Colt's words. Especially when he knew the other man was right. Jim was always thinking the worst. But didn't he have a right to? As far as he was concerned, life was meant to go wrong. It was meant to bring pain and suffering. A person couldn't escape those things entirely. But he could darned well do his best to detour around them whenever he had the chance.

Grimly, he turned back to the mare, but before

he untied her halter from the hitching post, he dug his phone from his shirt pocket and punched Tallulah's number.

She answered on the third ring. "Hi, Jim. What's up?"

The happy note in her voice made him wish he could be everything she needed him to be.

"Do you have a moment to talk or did I catch you at a bad time?"

"It's fine. I'm outside with the kids. They're riding their tricycles and pulling Maddie around in the wagon."

He shoved his hat back and wiped a forearm against his sweaty brow. "I'm calling to let you know I won't be home tonight. Colt needs for me to pull a shift of barn watch, and I couldn't very well turn him down."

"Of course you couldn't," she promptly replied. "But I have to say I'm disappointed."

"Yeah, well, I am, too."

"Are you?"

Surprised by her question, he tugged the brim of his hat back onto his forehead and stared blindly toward the opposite end of the barn.

"Why would you think anything else?"

There was a pause, and while he waited for her answer he could hear the children's happy squeals and shouts in the background. The sounds tore at him. Did the Hollister men realize just how fortunate they were? Even Holt, with the danger of losing his unborn child hanging over his head, was far more blessed than Jim. But that was petty thinking, he scolded himself. And he was above feeling sorry for himself.

"You haven't exactly been yourself, Jim."

"I admit I haven't been the life of the party. I'm sorry about that."

He was met with another stretch of silence, and then she said, "If you'd like, I can bring supper to the barn for you."

Seeing her would only make the helpless ache inside him even worse. "No. It's kind of you to offer, but I'll eat with the guys in the bunkhouse."

"Oh. Then I guess I'll see you whenever I see you. Bye, Jim."

The connection went dead, and as Jim slipped the phone back into his pocket, he wondered what his mother would say to him now. That he'd grown into the loser she'd always expected him to be?

Determined not to let the caustic question claw at him, Jim untied the mare's halter, then pulled a round peppermint from his pocket.

After he peeled the cellophane from the striped candy, he offered it to the horse. "There you go, Sugar. You deserve it for being such a good girl."

The mare happily chomped the peppermint before she turned her head and pressed her muzzle affectionately to Jim's cheek.

He patted her neck, while thinking how simple life would be if a piece of candy was all it would take to keep Tallulah by his side.

The next evening Tallulah took extra pains with her appearance before she drove over to see Jim, and as she made her way through the kitchen, Sophia didn't fail to notice her effort.

"Oh my, look at you! Your hair looks lovely with the top part pulled back. And that dress is hot, hot!"

Tallulah looked down at the blue-and-yellow printed sheath that clung to her figure. Other than the low rounded neckline and the crossed straps holding the upper back together, the garment was nothing close to fancy. But it might be sexy enough to grab Jim's attention and she was just woman enough to make him want to see what he was missing by not making love to her.

"I found it in town the other day and thought it would be cool. The summer heat is coming on fast. And so is your wedding," Tallulah said.

"Please don't say that word in this kitchen," Reeva called from her spot in front of the industrial-sized cookstove. "That's all I hear is wedding, wedding, wedding!"

Sophia's grandmother was obviously teasing, and Tallulah laughed while Sophia let out a good-natured groan.

"I can't help it," Sophia said. "Maureen is adding more guests to the list every day! Now she's saying she's hiring a five-piece band for the reception instead of a three-piece when a DJ would be fine for me. And she's planning to barbecue a whole steer, mind you! Along with ordering French champagne, she's having dozens and dozens of peonies and camellias brought in for decorations. And that's only a start! It's getting so out of hand I'm getting worried."

Laughing, Tallulah gave her friend's shoulders a gentle squeeze. "You're worrying for nothing. From what I hear, Maureen is an old hand at planning weddings. And she considers herself to be your second grandmother. It's going to be a beautiful day."

"That's exactly what I've told her," Reeva said, then turning away from the stove, she eyed Tallulah up and down. "Looks like you plan on scoring points with Jim tonight."

The smile instantly fell from Tallulah's face. "I don't know about that, Reeva. I just thought a new dress and a little makeup might help lift my spirits."

Reeva walked across the room and patted Tallulah's cheek. "Now, why would you need your spirits lifted? You have a good-looking, hardworking guy. And all the Hollisters love you. Same goes for me and Sophia. You ought to be happy."

Grateful for the cook's words of encouragement, Tallulah kissed her cheek.

"You're right, Reeva. Thank you for reminding me. Now, I'd better get going before Jim decides I've had a breakdown on the road."

Twenty minutes later, she arrived at Jim's house and after being apart from him the night before, she'd expected him to greet her with a hungry kiss.

Instead, he'd given her a half-hearted smile and invited her on to the kitchen. Doubts and questions whirled in her head as Tallulah followed him, but she kept them to herself. She'd already decided that tonight they needed to have a reckoning, but it could wait, she thought. At least, until after they'd eaten.

"I baked a frozen pizza. Hope that's okay with you," he said as he grabbed a mitten off the cabinet and peeked into the oven.

"You know me. I'll eat most anything." She walked over to the cabinets and pulled down plates and glasses. "And since you've been the cook, I'll set the table. Do you want beer or tea?"

"Beer. I'm tired as hell."

Tallulah was tired, too. Just not from physical labor. No, for the past several days she'd been fighting a mental battle with herself and the struggle had drained her. This uncertainty about Jim's moody behavior had to be resolved, one way or another.

Five minutes later they sat down to eat, and Tallulah did her best to appear hungry.

"You look beautiful tonight," he said as his gaze swept over her. "I should've taken you out to eat."

"I don't expect you to do that, Jim." Smiling faintly, she looked over at him. "How did the barn watch go? Have any trouble?"

"No. Everything was quiet. There are only a handful of mares that haven't yet foaled this year, but they're not due for a while."

"What if anyone of them had gone into labor?"

"Colt and Chandler handle the foaling." The corners of his lips turned downward. "I'm not experienced at bringing babies into the world."

Tallulah returned her tea glass to the table. "Speaking of babies, before I left the ranch house to come over here, Holt called Maureen with an update on Isabelle."

His head jerked up. "And?"

"Not much change. Except that Isabelle is yelling that she needs more food and wants to go home. So she must be feeling better."

"I imagine she does want to go home," he said with plenty of sarcasm. "But she needs to be thinking about her baby and keeping it safe."

Tallulah stared at him in amazement. "What do

you think she's been trying to do all these days? You're being a jerk, Jim. And I want to know why."

He put down his fork and lifted his face toward the ceiling. "Maybe because I'm just a natural-born jerk. Maybe because I can't be any other way."

Something was wrong with him, she decided. Something deep down in him was twisted. And unless he gave her a glimpse of the problem, there would be no chance of helping him.

"You can be flippant all you want, Jim. But I'm not stupid. Ever since this thing with Isabelle happened you've been in a dark hole. I'd like to help you get out of it, but you don't seem to want any help. Not from me."

The thought of taking one more bite of food sickened her, and she rose from the table and carried her plate over to the counter. As she scraped the uneaten pizza into the trash, Georgette came over and made a loving serpentine trail between her legs.

Too bad Jim hadn't learned to trust her the same way Georgette had, she thought, as she bent over and stroked the cat's back.

"Tallulah, I think…we…uh, need to talk."

She glanced up to see he was standing in front of her, and for one aching moment she wished she could simply walk into his arms and lay her head upon his strong chest. But making love to him wouldn't change anything. She'd already learned that sad fact.

Straightening away from the cat, she glared at him. "Couldn't you have come up with a better line than that? If you want to get rid of me, you should just come out and say it, Jim. I'm a big girl. I can take it. In fact, I've taken a lot worse than you've been dishing out. So don't feel like you have to handle me gently."

He grimaced. "I'm not trying to get rid of you! I'm only saying that I've been thinking about you and me. Us. And I don't like how I've been treating you. I don't like the way I've been feeling about myself—or anything else."

She could see real anguish on his face, and the sight of it broke her heart. "Why? If you don't tell me what's wrong, how do you expect me to help you fix it?"

He shook his head. "It can't be fixed. And I can't explain it. I just…can't."

She wanted to scream with frustration. "Are you feeling guilty about your late wife? Is that what this is about? You think it's selfish or wrong for you to be happy?"

"No! This has nothing to do with guilt or me thinking I'm betraying Lyndsey's memory."

Was he being totally honest? She searched his face for answers, but the dark shadows in his eyes told her nothing. Except that he was hurting.

"If that's true, then this has something to do with the baby, doesn't it?"

Cursing under his breath, he turned his back to her. "It always comes down to babies and children with you, Tallulah! And I—need for you to let it go. I can't talk about this. Don't ask me to."

His answer stunned her and for a long moment she didn't know how to respond.

Finally, she said, "Okay, Jim. You won't be bothered with my talk about children tonight, or any other time. In fact, you won't be bothered with me, period. All I can say is the next time you strike up an affair with a woman, just make sure she isn't a nanny."

Not bothering to wait on a response, she walked out of the kitchen and hurried through the house.

As she walked off the porch and out to her truck, she told herself she wasn't going to cry. She should be feeling proud of herself for avoiding a huge mistake with another man.

But as she drove away, the tears in her eyes turned the road ahead of her into a dark, watery trail.

Five days later, Jim was standing at the end of the training arena, mopping sweat from his face with a yellow bandanna when Luke rode up behind him.

For the past twenty minutes, the trainer had

been putting a gray gelding through a series of schooling exercises. Now, as Luke climbed down from the saddle, Jim could see both man and rider looked hot and tired.

"Finished with him?" Jim asked.

Luke nodded. "If it wasn't so darned hot, I would've kept going. But I don't want to get him overheated. Or myself."

Jim reached for the gelding's reins, which were dangling from Luke's hand. "I'll cool him down, then take him around to Farley for a bath."

When Luke didn't relinquish his hold on the reins, Jim arched a questioning brow at him. "What's the matter? I thought you were finished with the horse?"

"I am. But he can wait a minute. I want to talk to you."

Luke sounded firm and Jim braced himself. He wasn't ready for another of his coworkers to give him a lecture on his crappy mood. He'd already gotten enough of them from the guys in the bunkhouse. Their so-called friendly concern was beginning to grate on him.

"As long as the talk is about my job, I'm willing to stand here and listen. Otherwise, I don't want to hear a damned thing about my mood or the frown on my face. I just want to be left alone. Can't anyone around here understand that much?"

Luke smirked. "I'll tell you one thing, you're

about to get your wish to be alone, Jim. Because every guy on this ranch is ready to kick your ass!"

Jim didn't doubt the men were fed up with him. "Let them try it. I don't care."

"I'm beginning to wonder if you care about anything. Even yourself."

Jim wanted to tell him that he cared about himself least of all. But that revelation would only produce another lecture from Luke. One he wasn't ready to hear. And anyway, as far as he knew, Luke didn't know about Jim dating Tallulah or about their recent breakup. Which was surprising. Considering his brother Colt wasn't one to keep quiet.

"Look, Luke, I'm okay. I'm just worried about Holt and Isabelle, that's all. She's still in the hospital. That's not a good sign."

Frowning, Luke shook his head. "Isabelle's condition is stable. And the baby is healthy and growing. As long as they can stop her from delivering early, everything will be good. If you ask me, that's a good sign. And Holt has certainly remained positive and upbeat about the situation. You should, too."

Jim stared across the outdoor arena, but he wasn't seeing Colt trotting a little black filly in a huge circle or the white fluffy clouds scudding through the blue sky overhead. He wasn't hearing the distant bawl of weanling calves or the piercing cry of a hawk. He was hearing the hushed voices of the nurses as they worked over his infant son, who'd been far too weak to even utter a cry. He could hear the doctor saying if the baby's lungs would clear, if his heartbeat would grow stronger, if his kidneys continued to work...if, if, if.

Yes, there had been a time when Jim had summoned up every ounce of strength and courage he'd possessed to believe, to hope and hold on to anything positive. But being upbeat had done nothing to save his son.

"Jim? Did you hear me?"

Luke's sharp voice pierced his dismal thoughts, and he gave himself a hard mental shake before he looked at the man.

"Look Luke, I've been seeing Tallulah. Or I was—until I ruined things with her. And being without her isn't easy. But—she needs a man who isn't afraid to give her a child."

"And you are? Why?"

"Yeah. I'm afraid. And don't ask me why. I can't explain."

With a hopeless shake of his head, Luke handed the gelding's reins to Jim. "Here. I'm finished with the horse."

Jim watched the other man walk away, and for a few seconds he considered going after his friend. He wanted him to understand there were reasons for his bad behavior, deep reasons that were too painful to explain. But there was no use in going after Luke, he thought miserably. He couldn't talk to him about losing little Cody. No more than he'd been able to tell Tallulah what was in his heart.

"Look at this cow, Brody. She wants to be with the rest of the herd. You better get her and put her over here in the corral before she starts mooing," Tallulah told her little nephew.

For the past thirty minutes, Tallulah had been sitting in the middle of her brother's living room floor, helping the toddler create a maze of plastic fences around a group of barns and stables.

Giggling, the boy grabbed up the plastic Hereford cow and held it out to Tallulah. "Moo! Moo! She cry. See?"

"Oh, no. You don't want her to cry." Tallulah pointed to one of the corrals they'd already filled with several more plastic cows. "Put her over here where she can find her baby calf. Then she'll be happy."

Brody seemed to think her idea was a good one. He was plunking the cow into the tiny corral when Taggart and Emily-Ann walked into the room.

"Hey, sis, come have a cup of coffee with me," he said. "Emily-Ann needs to play with Brody for a while."

"Cows, Dada! Moo-moo!"

He affectionately rubbed the top of Brody's red

head. "I see lots of cows. And Mommy is going to help you keep them all rounded up."

"That's right. I'm the official cowgirl around here. I know how to keep cowboys and cattle rounded up," Emily-Ann playfully announced as she sank to the floor next to her son.

Taggart reached for Tallulah's hand. "Come on," he said. "Emily-Ann brought home raspberry jam doughnuts from Conchita's."

He pulled her up from the floor and as Tallulah walked with him to the kitchen, she asked, "Is this a conspiracy to get me away from my nephew?"

He chuckled. "Not hardly. You'll have plenty more time to spend with Brody after we have our coffee."

This evening was the first time in a long while that she'd had dinner with her brother and sister-in-law. Before, her nights had been monopolized with Jim. But that had all changed five days ago.

And in spite of trying to put on a good front for everyone, she'd never felt so adrift or lost in her life.

"Sit down and let me do the serving." Taggart motioned to a breakfast bar that created an L at the end of the cabinets.

"Wow! Married life has changed you," she teased as she took a seat on one of the tall bar-stools. "My macho brother serving me coffee and doughnuts. Who would've thought?"

He grinned as he placed two cups of coffee onto the bar. "It's great to have you here tonight, Lulah. Since you took the job as the Hollisters' nanny, we've not really spent much time together."

Taggart was the only person in the world to call her by the shortened name, and it reminded her of when the two of them had been very young children and they'd huddled together while their father had thrown his many drunken fits. Being four years older than Tallulah, her brother had always been her protector. And because Buck O'Brien had mostly been an absent husband and father, Taggart had shouldered the responsibility of trying to make life better for her and their mother.

"I know. But it's not going to be like that anymore," she said, then gave him a wan smile. "That is, until Kat delivers her twins. Then I expect I'll be very busy for a long while."

He carried a plate of doughnuts over to the counter and placed them in front of her, then took a seat next to her.

"You're looking forward to the twins being born, aren't you?"

"Oh yes. Kat plans to take eight weeks off work after the babies are born. Once she returns to her job, I can be a stand-in mom to two infants at the same time, while juggling the care of five older children. It's going to be a fun challenge. But if things get too hectic Jazelle and Sophia will be around to help me."

"I'm glad. I've been worried that you might end up getting tired of dealing with little people all day." He picked up one of the doughnuts and demolished a third of it with one bite. "But you've always been good with kids. I just wish you had one or two of your own."

She cut a glance in his direction. "Why do you say that? You know how things turned out with Shane. And even if we hadn't divorced, he was opposed to having children. Of course we were into several months of marriage before I found out how the guy really felt about being a father."

Taggart frowned at her. "Why are you bringing up Shane?"

"You just now said you wished I had children of my own. And Shane is the only husband I've had." Shrugging, she reached for one of the doughnuts before Taggart started pestering her about eating one. "I understand some women have babies and remain single, and that's fine if that's what they choose. It's just not my style."

"No. It's not your style. Your style is a home and husband. And Emily-Ann and I thought you were headed in that direction. Now I hear that you and Jim have parted ways. Want to tell me what happened?"

Wanting to appear indifferent, she shrugged.

"Why bother hearing the details? It's over and done with."

He sipped his coffee before he settled a pointed look on her. "This is your brother, Lulah. Don't try to fool me. All I have to do is look into your eyes to see that you're hurting. During dinner, it was obvious you were putting on a happy act for us. But you know what, you bomb as an actress."

Tallulah grimaced. "Sorry. You know how I always hated speech class and those horrible plays Mrs. Barstow had us doing."

He grunted with amusement. "Actually, you did a pretty good job when you played that part of the wicked witch. I think it came naturally."

"Thanks, brother."

He reached over and patted her forearm. "You know I'm kidding. You also know that I want you to be happy. And when I first heard about you and Jim, I was thrilled. He's a good man. And a hard-working man."

The brave front that Tallulah had been trying to present to everyone, especially Taggart, suddenly crumbled and she dropped her face in her hands to hide her tears.

"Yes, I know Jim is all that, Tag. And I—I might as well be honest. I'm crazy in love with the guy. But he…uh…doesn't want anything serious. Not from me or any woman. I think he believes he's incapable of being a husband and father. That he doesn't have the ability to love."

"Why not?"

Dropping her hands, she reached for a napkin in a nearby holder and dabbed at the tears on her cheeks. "You should know, Tag. You lost your wife and baby to a car crash. Well, Jim lost his wife to a horse accident. Since then he's turned his back on having a family."

Taggart blew out a heavy breath. "Yes. I knew that Jim was a widower. And I won't try to sugar-coat things, Tallulah. I went through hell trying to move on and find love again. If Emily-Ann hadn't forced me to open my eyes, I might still be living in a shell. One thing for sure, you can't give up on him, sis. You need to keep fighting. If he cares anything at all for you, he'll eventually lose his blinders."

Fighting? How was a woman supposed to fight against a stone wall? "I'm not so sure. He said some unforgivable things."

It always comes down to babies and children with you, Tallulah! And I—need for you to let it go. I can't talk about this. Don't ask me to.

Now that she'd had time to think about Jim's outburst, she was even more perplexed by it. If he disliked children that much, then why was he so worried about Holt's unborn baby?

Frowning thoughtfully, she looked at her

brother. "I don't understand him, Tag. He seems overly cut up about Isabelle and the baby. It doesn't make sense. He says it's because Holt is like a brother to him. But I think it's something more."

"Well, I'm sure that Holt is like a brother to him. Jim has been here on Three Rivers much longer than me."

"He told me he's been here on the ranch for nine years," Tallulah said.

"That's a long time. And he works closely with Holt six or seven days of the week. No doubt it worries Jim to think Holt might lose his baby. But then, it's worrying all of us."

"Yes."

Taggart leaned over and curled his arm around her shoulders. "Would you like for me to have a talk with Jim? Maybe if he knew how I lost Becca and the baby it would help him to see that life goes on."

"No! I don't want you to intervene for me. Besides, he knows about you. He mentioned to me once about you being a widower before you married Emily-Ann. Besides, he can see that people around him have suffered losses and yet moved on with their lives."

"Hmm. Sounds like you got a real mule head on your hands."

"Just please don't say anything to him, Tag. If Jim ever does decide he wants to try again with me, I want it to be a decision he made on his own. Not because he was pushed."

"Mules are far different than horses. Mules have to be pushed. Just ask Holt," he said, then suddenly as if a light bulb had switched on, he snapped his fingers. "I got it now!"

She cast him a wary glance. "Got what?"

"Nothing. Nothing at all." Shaking his head, he pointed to her doughnut. "Eat up. And we'll go see if Brody has all his cows rounded up."

Smiling wanly, she reached over and squeezed his hand. "Will you ever quit trying to take care of me?"

He grinned. "Maybe. Whenever you get a husband who loves you as much as I do. Then I'll hand the job over to him."

More tears burned her eyes, but she managed to stop them from falling onto her cheeks.

"I'm afraid, dear brother, you're going to be stuck with the job for a long time."

Because try as she might, Tallulah could never see herself loving any man, except Jim.

Chapter Eleven

The next day, Jim was in the mares' paddock, checking to see if any of them needed their hooves trimmed, when Farley walked up to him.

Considering that Farley rarely ventured this far away from the barn, Jim was surprised to see the ginger-haired cowboy.

"What are you doing out here, Farley? Run out of something to do?"

"No. I have a pile of work waiting on me. I came out here to tell you that Holt wants to see you in his office. Now."

Jim frowned. "Holt? Why didn't he send me a text instead of running you all over creation?"

"He did. You must not have gotten it. So he found me at the horse bath and told me to go find you."

Jim pulled out his phone to see if there was an

unread message from Holt. There wasn't, but that was hardly surprising. Sometimes the phone signal was spotty on certain areas of the ranch.

"No message. Okay, Farley. Thanks. I'll go see him right now."

Holt hadn't shown up at the ranch at all yesterday, and Colt and Luke weren't expecting him to make an appearance today. Something must have happened to change his plans, Jim decided.

With that uneasy thought in mind, he headed to the horse barn.

Inside the massive structure, Jim found the door to Holt's office open and after knocking on the outer wall, he stepped into the room.

Holt was sitting at his desk with the landline phone jammed to his ear. The smile on his face assured Jim that the situation with Isabelle and the baby hadn't worsened. A fact that gave him a measure of relief.

As soon as Holt spotted Jim, he pointed to one of the wooden chairs in front of his desk and quickly ended the phone conversation.

"Sit down, Jim. I see Farley found you."

Jim nodded. "I was in the mares' paddock. A few of them need their hooves trimmed. I'm going to get to that this afternoon."

"No. You're not going to be trimming any hooves this afternoon. In fact, you're not going to be working at all."

Jim's jaw dropped. "I'm not? What are you planning to do? Fire me?"

Holt frowned. "I ought to fire you just for being stupid."

Jim didn't know whether to laugh or curse as he scooted to the edge of the seat. "Am I supposed to know what you're talking about? I wasn't aware that I'd done anything wrong."

"There isn't anything wrong with your work, Jim. You're one of the best hands Three Rivers has, or ever will have."

Holt's compliment should've put a smile on his face, but it didn't. Nor did it stem the questions racing through his mind.

"Thanks for that much, Holt. But I don't understand. That doesn't explain what this is about. What have I done to make me such a chump?" he asked, then before Holt could respond, Jim was struck with the awful answer. "Oh. I should have guessed already. The men have been complaining to you about me. Well, I don't blame them. I've been a horse's ass around here."

"Since I've had to be away from the ranch so much here lately, I couldn't say what you've been. But I'll take your word for it." He dismissed Jim's confession with a shrug. "For your information the men haven't been griping to me. The problem I'm having with you is your thick, mule head. You've let the best thing that could've possibly happened to you get away. No. Get away isn't right. More like you pushed her away."

Rising from his desk, Holt went over to a table loaded with a coffee machine and an assortment of snacks, and Jim watched in amazement as he filled a mug with dark liquid from a stainless-steel carafe.

Holt was scolding him about Tallulah? He couldn't believe it! "What are you talking about? No, forget that. I want to know who's been talking to you. Colt?"

"Why are you picking on him?" Holt asked.

"He's mouthy, that's why."

"And you're not mouthy enough," Holt retorted. "And just so you'll know, Colt hasn't said a word about this to me."

Feeling like a bug crawling on the floor, Jim lifted his hat and shoved a hand through his hair. "I sound like a real jerk, don't I?"

Holt sipped his coffee before he answered. "You sure do. But sometimes when a man falls in love he tends to go a little haywire."

Jim scrubbed his face with both hands as Holt's words rattled around in his head. Yes, he'd gone haywire. And so far nothing had righted itself in his mind. He'd believed putting some time and space between him and Tallulah would help him return to the man he'd been before he'd met her.

But being apart from her had only shown Jim how much he loved her.

Bending his head, he continued to rub fingers across his forehead. "You're right, Holt. I do love Tallulah. She's an incredible woman. That's why I want her to be happy. She deserves to have a man who can give her what she wants. Love and children."

"You can't give her those things?"

"The love, yeah. But not the children. And you know how she feels about kids. Hell, she's a nanny!"

Frowning, Holt returned to his seat behind the desk. "Why can't you give her children? Do you have a medical problem, or something?"

Jim could feel his face turning red. Over the years, he'd discussed many subjects with Holt, but nothing this private.

"No! I don't have medical issues in that department. I...just don't want children in my life."

Holt was far from convinced. "Why? Little ones get on your nerves?"

"Like fingernails on a blackboard."

"Liar. I've watched you interact with my sons. I got the impression that you love those boys. And I don't think I could be that wrong about you."

Jim's throat was suddenly so tight he could hardly breathe. "Okay, so I'm lying," he said roughly, then quickly rose from the chair. "Sorry, Holt, but I don't want to talk about this anymore."

He started toward the door, but Holt was faster and Jim watched in dismay as the other man closed the door, preventing him from making an escape.

"I'm sorry, too, Jim. I don't normally butt into my friends' private lives. I figure that's their own personal business. But I care about you too much to stand by and do nothing while you mess things up. I want you to be happy. I want Tallulah to be happy."

"It's no good, Holt. You don't understand."

"No. I won't understand until you explain." He gestured to the chair Jim had vacated moments ago. "Go sit down. I want to hear everything."

Seeing no way out of this, Jim returned to the chair. Holt took a seat in the matching wooden chair and, crossing his arms over his chest, waited for Jim to speak.

Drawing in a deep breath, Jim said, "This isn't a good time for this. But since you want to know…"

"Go on."

"When I first came here to Three Rivers, I told you about Lyndsey and how she'd died. But I didn't tell you everything." He met Holt's keen gaze. "At the time of the accident she was seven months pregnant with our child."

If the revelation shocked Holt, it didn't show

on his face. His expression remained unchanged as he continued to regard Jim. "What happened?"

"Before Lyndsey died, the doctors performed a C-section in an effort to save the baby. It was a boy. He was fully developed and under normal circumstances would've survived. But the baby had suffered injuries and ended up living for only six days."

After a moment Holt grimaced and said, "I'm really sorry this happened to you, Jim. You've obviously gone through hell."

"Yeah, that's one way of putting it," he muttered.

"Well, I'm really glad you shared this with me," Holt told him. "Because now I know I'm right in calling you stupid."

Jim didn't know what he'd been expecting from Holt, but this reaction knocked him for a loop.

"Okay, Holt, I apologize. With what you're going through right now with Isabelle, you didn't need to hear about my baby son dying. It was bad, bad timing. But you kept pushing me to explain and—"

"Damn it, Jim, hearing about your son doesn't make me worry any more about Isabelle! But it makes me worry a whole lot less about you. Because now I see that you don't have a problem. The only thing you need to be concerned about is finding the guts to face Tallulah and tell her you've been a fool."

Jim's mouth fell open. "You still don't understand, Holt. I can't give Tallulah children. I can't take the risk of losing another child. Of going through that much pain again."

"You don't exactly look like a ball of joy right now," he said in a sardonic voice. "And what makes you think you'd lose another child? Could be you might have five or six without a problem."

Jim shook his head. "How can you sound so upbeat, Holt? When Isabelle is in the hospital and—"

"I can be upbeat because I happen to think being positive makes everything better. And Isabelle is doing fine. So is the baby. She's in the hospital because the doctor knows if he lets her out, she'll end up doing too much. And frankly, I agree with him."

Holt stood and slapped a comforting hand on Jim's shoulder. "Don't get me wrong, Jim. I'm sorry as heck that you lost your son. But life goes on and yes, it involves taking risks. But you have a chance to start over. Tallulah will give you the love and children you deserve. All you have to do is give her the chance."

Doubts swirled through him as he looked warily up at Holt. "Convincing Tallulah that I'm not a mule head might not be easy."

Holt grinned. "Nothing good ever comes easy.

Now get out of here. And I don't want to find you back in this barn until tomorrow morning."

"Tallulah, there's someone here to see you," Sophia said. "He's waiting on the back steps."

From a seat at the kitchen table, Tallulah glanced up to see the young cook was standing a few feet behind her left shoulder.

"He?"

She knew for certain that Taggart was working out on a far range today with a bunch of the ranch hands. God help her, surely Buck O'Brien hadn't found his way to Three Rivers. In her current state of mind, he was the last thing she needed to deal with.

"Jim," Sophia answered with a smug smile.

What was *he* doing here? Hadn't he hurt her enough?

She glanced around the table at the five kids, all of them happily chomping on pieces of fresh fruit and cheese slices.

"I can't leave the kids."

"Don't even start," Sophia warned. "I'll watch the kids."

Her heart racing, Tallulah rose to her feet and brushed the cracker crumbs from the front of her blue jeans.

"Don't worry, Sophia, this won't take long," she said grimly.

"I hope it takes a long, long time," Sophia told her as she shooed her away from the table.

At the back door of the kitchen, Tallulah drew in a bracing breath before she opened it and stepped onto the small porch.

Jim was standing on the top step looking out toward the open rangeland that swept toward the part of the ranch where Taggart's house was located. As soon as he heard the door close behind her, he looked around and Tallulah's knees turned to sponge as soon as her gaze met his.

"Hello, Tallulah."

Her eyes narrowed skeptically as her heartbeat grew so rapid and shallow she thought she might faint. "What are you doing here?" she asked bluntly.

"I'm here because…I need to talk with you. Can you spare me a few minutes?"

A part of her wanted to tell him to get lost and go pull some other woman's emotions wrong side out. And yet just the sight of him made her spirits fly like a bird that had been caged for far too long.

"Don't you think we talked enough the other night? Aren't you afraid I might slip and say the word baby or child?" she asked caustically.

He stepped up onto the porch to stand in front of her, and the close-up version of Jim very nearly took her breath. Why did he have to be so damned handsome? So ruggedly masculine from his feet to the very top of his tawny hair?

"I deserve that and more. I've been all kinds of a fool. And I'm sorry."

"You said that before, but nothing changed with you."

He took off his hat and gave it a helpless swat against the side of his leg. "You're right. I didn't change because I thought…it would be hopeless to try."

"And now?"

He gently reached for her hand and slid his fingers between hers. "Please come sit on the patio with me."

She couldn't have resisted him even if she'd wanted to. "All right," she said quietly.

Once they reached the patio, he pulled out a chair at the table where they'd first had dinner together, and as he helped Tallulah into the seat, she tried not to think of that night and how charmed she'd been by him. She also tried not to hope that some sort of cataclysmic occurrence had taken place in him and he'd decided the two of them should and would be together. From now until forever.

"Now, what is this about, Jim? Because I'll be frank. I don't intend to pick up where we left off. It wouldn't work. Not for me."

He sat in the chair next to hers, then scooted it so close their knees were touching.

"I don't want to pick up where we ended the other night. That wasn't good for me, either. I want us to start over completely," he said. Reaching for both her hands, he held them tightly. "I want you to understand the demons I've been living with and believe that I'm finally ready to put them behind me."

From the moment she'd walked onto the porch and saw him standing there, hope had been knocking on the door of her heart. Up until this moment, she'd refused to let it in. But now she couldn't stop it from pouring through her like a hot ray of sunshine.

"Demons?"

His expression solemn, he nodded. "You were right. When I heard that Isabelle's pregnancy was troubled—well, everything came back to me. The memories slapped me in the face so hard that I couldn't push them aside. And then each time I looked at you, each time we made love I was terrified to think it all might happen again."

Shaking her head, she asked, "What might happen again?"

He swallowed, then said, "I had a son who lived for six short days, Tallulah. I got to hold him in my arms just a few brief times before he died."

Stunned, her mind whirled with questions.

"Lyndsey was carrying your baby when the accident happened?"

"Yes. She was seven months into her pregnancy. Baby Cody was fully developed, but too injured to survive. I was never able to get over the loss. Somehow losing him was even worse than losing Lyndsey. After he died, I swore I'd never put myself in the position where I could lose another child."

Tears sprang to her eyes and rolled onto her cheeks. "Oh, Jim, why didn't you tell me? I needed to understand. I wanted to understand, but you kept shutting me out."

"I know. But I couldn't bring myself to tell you. Besides being painful to talk about, I didn't want you to think I was an emotional weakling." His lips twisted to a wry slant. "Instead, I made myself look like something far worse—a jackass."

"All this time I was thinking…well, that you wanted to call it quits because you didn't love me," she said in hushed voice. "And maybe you don't. I don't know. But—"

Her words broke off as he suddenly drew her up from the chair and pulled her into his arms. "Oh, Tallulah, I don't know whether you love me, either. But I want to believe that you love me as much as I love you."

Closing her teary eyes, she pressed her cheek against his chest. "You haven't been the only one who's behaved like a fool, Jim. I think…all along I was afraid to tell you how much I loved you. I didn't want to be that vulnerable and put myself in a position to be hurt by another man. And then when we parted, I had to face the fact that I'd failed again and that I was hurting anyway."

Resting his cheek against the top of her head, he stroked fingers through her hair. "We're going to put all of this behind us, Tallulah."

With his hands cupping her jaws, he tilted her face up to his. "Holt just told me something that makes me very glad I'm alive and holding you in my arms."

"And what was that?"

"He said that you would give me love and babies. Was he right?"

She smiled with all the joy and love that was bursting in her heart. "Absolutely right. But are you sure about the babies part?"

His arms slipped around her back and drew her tight against him. "I want us to have a full life together, Tallulah. I want to be a father and you to be a mother. I want a real family. Yes, having kids involves risk. We're seeing Holt going through those trials right now. But loving you has made me see that a person has to take those risks if he wants the real rewards of life."

Her face wreathed in happiness, she took his hand and placed the palm upon her forehead. "Do

I have a fever? I think I might be hallucinating," she softly teased.

Chuckling now, he began to press kisses over her cheeks and chin and forehead. "You don't have a fever, my darling. But I'm going to make sure you stay plenty warm tonight—in my bed and my arms."

"For always," she whispered, then catching his face between her hands, she pulled his mouth down to hers.

Epilogue

The fourth Saturday in June turned out to be perfect weather for an early-evening wedding on Three Rivers Ranch. With the setting sun spreading pink and golden hues across the huge yard in front of the ranch house and a cool breeze ruffling the leaves of the cottonwoods, Sophia and Colt exchanged their vows beneath an archway of camellias, peonies and roses in shades ranging from the palest pink to dark magenta. Standing by Colt's side, his brother, Luke, served as best man, while Sophia had chosen Jazelle to be her matron of honor.

Sophia's mother had stubbornly refused to attend her daughter's wedding, but her grandmother, Reeva, more than made up for the absent parent. Tallulah had never seen the older woman looking so lovely in a long floral dress and her salt-and-pepper hair coiled into an intricate chignon.

Sheldon Vandale had traveled all the way from California to do the honor of handing his daughter over to the groom, and his presence had made the day even more special for Sophia.

By the time the officiating minister pronounced the couple man and wife and the newly married couple was swallowed up by the wedding guests, Tallulah was desperately fishing a tissue from her purse.

Jim watched with dismay as she dabbed the white square to her weeping eyes.

"Tallulah, you shouldn't be crying. You've been looking forward to this day for months. And Sophia and Colt are over the moon happy. It's all great."

Shaking her head, she gave him a hopeless smile. "It's a sentimental tradition, sweetheart. A woman is supposed to cry at weddings."

Wrapping his arm through hers, he slowly led her away from the group of well-wishers who continued to monopolize the new bride and groom.

"I hope you're not planning on crying at our wedding," he joked. "People will think becoming my wife is going to make you miserable."

"I'd rather be put in chains and fed bread and water," she teased, then leaned up on her tiptoes to kiss his cheek.

A week after Jim and Tallulah had reunited that day on the patio, he'd presented her with an oval-shaped diamond solitaire mounted on a gold antique setting. Nearly three months had passed since then, and she was still enchanted with the beautiful engagement ring. And even more in love with Jim than the day he'd proposed.

Now they were planning a fall wedding, which had to be after Katherine and Blake's twins arrived in late August or early September, and before the foaling season started in late November. Since Tallulah had lost her own mother years before, Maureen was more than happy to be her stand-in mom, and the Hollister matriarch was already promising to give Tallulah and Jim a wedding as big and beautiful as Sophia and Colt's.

"Hey, you two, the bride and groom are the only ones allowed to be kissing around here," Holt playfully scolded as he walked up to join them.

"Where's Isabelle?" Jim asked. "I'm going to ask her if you've been sticking to these no kissing rules."

Holt laughed. "She's already raced into the house to check on our new son. I'm not sure if Isabelle fusses over little Wes the most, or if Mom is the guiltiest." Pausing, he shook his head. "No, I probably have that all wrong. Gabby might be the worst mother hen of them all."

Two weeks ago and right on schedule, Isabelle had delivered a healthy baby boy they had named Weston Langford after great-grandparents on both sides of the family. And Jim had proudly accepted the honor of being the child's godfather.

Jim chuckled knowingly. "Who are you kidding, Holt? You're the biggest mother hen of them all. I'll be surprised if you make it past the first champagne toast before you head for the house."

Holt grinned from ear to ear. "You know, it's funny because all the while Isabelle was pregnant with this baby, I had the notion that I wanted a girl. When he turned out to be a boy, I was ecstatic. I'm a man with three sons! What could be better?"

"Maybe a girl to go with them?" Tallulah suggested with a clever smile.

Laughing, Holt patted her cheek before he leveled a sly look at Jim.

"Sounds like you have your work cut out for you."

Jim's arm tightened around the back of Tallulah's waist. "That's what happens when a man falls in love with a nanny," he told him.

Holt was still laughing when Chandler walked up to his brother and gently slapped him on the arm.

"Sorry, you two," the veterinarian apologized to Jim and Tallulah. "I need to borrow the life of the party for a few minutes. There's a guest in the crowd who's interested in a buying a horse."

As the brothers walked away, Tallulah turned to Jim. "Do the Hollister men ever quit being ranchers, even for a few minutes?"

"Oh, they have their moments," Jim said slyly.

"How do you think they produced all the little Hollisters you've been taking care of?"

She feigned a puzzled look. "Hmm. I wonder."

Kissing her cheek, he turned her toward a group of guests filing toward the back of the house. "Come on," he urged. "You can wonder while we walk to the patio for the reception."

Minutes later, as Jim and Tallulah stood at the edge of the crowd, drinking champagne from fluted glasses, Emily-Ann and Camille strolled up to them.

Since Camille and Matthew had driven up two days ago from Red Bluff, the two redheads had been visiting up a storm. And it warmed Tallulah's heart to see her sister-in-law enjoying this special time with her best friend.

"Your mother has done it again," Jim told the youngest Hollister sibling. He gestured toward the massive crowd gathered on the patio and adjoining yard. "This is quite a blowout."

Laughing at his description, Camille said, "Mother loves putting on blowouts. So you two might as well get ready for yours. But for now I'm worried she might just be stirring up a big blow *up*."

Jim and Tallulah exchanged curious glances.

"Did you say blow up?" Tallulah asked. "Is anything wrong?"

Before Camille could explain, Emily-Ann spoke

up. "We won't know if anything is wrong until the truth comes out. Right, Camille?"

"Truth about what?" Jim questioned.

Camille rolled her eyes over to where Maureen and Gil stood with their heads close together. The couple always appeared to be deliriously in love with each other, so Tallulah knew there was no problem brewing between those two.

"Since the Hollister family is growing in leaps and bounds, Mother decided it was time for her to make a family tree," Camille said. "We all agreed it was a good idea. Until she announced to us yesterday that she thinks she's found another branch of Hollisters. Ones we didn't know existed."

"Somewhere in Utah," Emily-Ann added succinctly.

Amazed by this news, Tallulah asked, "She actually believes these other Hollisters might be your relatives?"

Seemingly unconvinced, Camille shrugged. "She's leaning toward the possibility. But I have my doubts."

"Maureen is in the process of trying to parley a meeting with these other Hollisters."

Camille shot Emily-Ann a droll look. "Parley, heck! She's going to invite them to come here to Three Rivers!"

"Would that be so bad?" Tallulah questioned.

"Maybe not. But what if these people are a bunch

of gold diggers, or con artists, or just generally creepy?" Camille voiced her concerns. "They're strangers and we have no idea yet if they're actually related to us."

Jim smiled. "And what if they're genuinely good people? You might want to know they're your relatives."

Before Camille could answer his question, Vivian walked up with an anxious look on her face. "Finally, sissy! I've been looking all over this crowd for you!"

"Why? Is the nanny having problems with Carter?"

"No. Nothing like that." She wrapped a hand around Camille's arm. "You're needed in the kitchen. The catering people are having a meltdown over something."

Camille glanced ruefully at Jim and Tallulah. "I leave my diner in Dragoon to spend my time up here in the kitchen!" she joked, then curled a forefinger at Emily-Ann. "Come on. You can help, too."

As the three women hurried away, Jim said, "I hope the temporary nanny Maureen hired for today doesn't have a meltdown. Because I don't want to give you up for one minute. We have lots of dancing to do."

Tallulah cast him an impish glance. "Really? You know how to dance?"

"It's been a while," he said with a wry grin.

"But I think I can manage to whirl you around the floor."

"We'll see!" she said happily, and then her expression grew serious as she reached for his hand and held it tightly in hers. "Jim, do you think Maureen is making a mistake by getting involved with these *other* Hollisters?"

He shrugged. "Time will tell, I suppose. But I know one thing for sure. I'm a happy man for getting involved with you."

The love in his voice filled Tallulah's heart, and she couldn't stop herself from tilting her lips invitingly up to his.

"Oh no," he teased. "You're asking me to break the rules. Holt said no kissing."

Chuckling, Tallulah stood on tiptoes to bring her face closer to his. "What does he know about it?"

Smiling, Jim inched his lips down to hers. "The man has three sons. He ought to know a thing or two about kissing. And one of these days, my beautiful darling, we might have three sons of our own."

"I can hardly wait," she murmured.

And as his lips came down on hers, Tallulah knew the stars behind her eyes and the birds singing in her ears would never go away whenever he kissed her. Just like their love for each other would never fade.

* * * * *

**WE HOPE YOU ENJOYED
THIS BOOK FROM**

⬦ HARLEQUIN
SPECIAL
EDITION

Believe in love. Overcome obstacles. Find happiness.

Relate to finding comfort and strength in the
support of loved ones and enjoy the journey
no matter what life throws your way.

6 NEW BOOKS AVAILABLE EVERY MONTH!

HSEHALO2020

#2899 CINDERELLA NEXT DOOR
The Fortunes of Texas: The Wedding Gift
by Nancy Robards Thompson

High school teacher and aspiring artist Ginny Sanders knows she is not Draper Fortune's type. Content to admire her fabulous and flirty new neighbor from a distance, she is stunned when he asks her out. Draper is charmed by the sensitive teacher, but when he learns why she doesn't date, he must decide if he can be the man she needs...

#2900 HEIR TO THE RANCH
Dawson Family Ranch • by Melissa Senate

The more Gavin Dawson shirks his new role, the more irate Lily Gold gets. The very pregnant single mom-to-be is determined to make her new boss see the value in his late father's legacy—her livelihood and her home depend on it! But Gavin's plan to ignore his inheritance and Lily—*and* his growing attraction to her—is proving to be impossible...

#2901 CAPTIVATED BY THE COWGIRL
Match Made in Haven • by Brenda Harlen

Devin Blake is a natural loner, but when rancher Claire Lamontagne makes the first move, he finds himself wondering if he's as content as he thought he was. Is Devin ready to trade his solitary life for a future with the cowgirl tempting him to take a chance on love?

#2902 MORE THAN A TEMPORARY FAMILY
Furever Yours • by Marie Ferrarella

A visit with family was just what Josie Whitaker needed to put her marriage behind her. Horseback-riding lessons were an added bonus. But her instructor, Declan Hoyt, is dealing with his moody teenage niece. The divorced single mom knows just how to help and offers to teach Declan a thing or two about parenting—never expecting a romance to spark with the younger rancher!

#2903 LAST CHANCE ON MOONLIGHT RIDGE
Top Dog Dude Ranch • by Catherine Mann

Their love wasn't in doubt, but fertility issues and money problems have left Hollie and Jacob O'Brien's marriage in shambles. So once the spring wedding season at their Tennessee mountain ranch is over, they'll part ways. Until Jacob is inspired to romance Hollie and her long-buried maternal instincts are revived by four orphaned children visiting the ranch. Will their future together be resurrected, too?

#2904 AN UNEXPECTED COWBOY
Sutton's Place • by Shannon Stacey

Lone-wolf cowboy Irish is no stranger to long, lonely nights. But somehow Mallory Sutton tugs on his heartstrings. The feisty single mom is struggling to balance it all—and challenging Irish's perception of what he has to offer. But will their unexpected connection keep Irish in town...or end in heartbreak for Mallory and her kids?

"You still don't belong here." Mariella crossed her arms
over her chest, and Alex commanded himself not to notice
her body, perfect as it was.

"That makes two of us, and yet here we are."

"I was here first," she muttered. He'd heard the argument
before, but it didn't sway him.

"You're not running me off, Mariella. I needed a fresh
start, and this is the place I've picked for my home."

"My plan was to leave the past behind me. You are a
physical reminder of so many mistakes I've made."

"I can't say that upsets me too much," he lied. It didn't
make sense, but he hated that he made her so uncomfortable.
Hated even more that sometimes he'd purposely drive by

her shop to get a glimpse of her through the picture window. Talk about a glutton for punishment.

She let out a low growl. "You are an infuriating man. Stubborn and callous. I don't even know if you have a heart."

"Funny." He kept his voice steady even as memories flooded him, making his head pound. "That's the rationale Amber gave me for why she cheated with your fiancé. My lack of emotions pushed her into his arms. What was his excuse?"

She looked out at the street for nearly a minute, and Alex wondered if she was even going to answer. He followed her gaze to the park across the street, situated in the center of the town. There were kids at the playground and several families walking dogs on the path that circled the perimeter. Magnolia was the perfect place to raise a family.

If a person had the heart to be that kind of a man—the type who married the woman he loved and set out to be a good husband and father. Alex wasn't cut out for a family, but he liked it in the small coastal town just the same.

"I was too committed to my job," she said suddenly and so quietly he almost missed it.

"Ironic since it was your job that introduced him to Amber."

"Yeah." She made a face. "This is what I'm talking about, Alex. A past I don't want to revisit."

"Then stay away from me, Mariella," he advised. "Because I'm not going anywhere."

"Then maybe I will," she said and walked away.

Don't miss
Wedding Season *by Michelle Major,*
available May 2022 wherever
HQN books and ebooks are sold.

HQNBooks.com